FLAMES OF DECEIT

FLAMES OF DECEIT

LORETTA JACKSON

THORNDIKE
CHIVERS

This Large Print edition is published by Thorndike Press, Waterville, Maine, USA and by BBC Audiobooks Ltd, Bath, England.

Thorndike Press is an imprint of Thomson Gale, a part of The Thomson Corporation.

Thorndike is a trademark and used herein under license.

The text of this Large Print edition is unabridged.

Other aspects of the book may vary from the original edition.

Set in 16 pt. Plantin.

LIBRARY OF CONGRESS CATALOGING-IN-PUBLICATION DATA

Jackson, Loretta.
    Flames of deceit / by Loretta Jackson.
      p. cm. — (Thorndike Press large print candlelight)
    ISBN-13: 978-0-7862-9519-7 (alk. paper)
    ISBN-10: 0-7862-9519-8 (alk. paper)
    1. Arson investigation — Fiction. 2. Kansas — Fiction. 3. Large type
books. I. Title.
PS3560.A224F57 2007
813'.54—dc22   2007002310

BRITISH LIBRARY CATALOGUING-IN-PUBLICATION DATA AVAILABLE

Published in 2007 in the U.S. by arrangement with Loretta Jackson.
Published in 2007 in the U.K. by arrangement with the author.

U.K. Hardcover: 978 1 405 64216 3 (Chivers Large Print)
U.K. Softcover: 978 1 405 64217 0 (Camden Large Print)

Printed in the United States of America on permanent paper
10 9 8 7 6 5 4 3 2 1

To sister Vickie Britton, faithful friend
and writing partner.

With special thanks to Ed Britton
for the original cover art.

CHAPTER 1

Apprehension gripped Sonya as she glimpsed Uncle Alex's house, rising like an antebellum mansion from the gently rolling Kansas plain. Despite the sturdy row of columns, the long front porch seemed to sag. Paint peeled in places, revealing the naked gray-brown boards beneath. The Rathmell Place, as people still called it, no longer possessed the look of aloof nobility, but now seemed marred, on the brink of decay.

Sonya had talked to Dan Rathmell, Uncle Alex's stepson, on the phone before she'd left Boston. He'd tried to prepare her. "Everything's changed," he'd said, an edge to his voice. "Alex has made a bad mistake, remarrying again so soon after my mother died."

"Uncle Alex is all right, isn't he? He's recovering from the stroke?"

"He's fine, but nothing else is. I'm afraid

this time he's got mixed up with some real con artists. But you'll be able to judge for yourself soon. How long will you be able to stay?"

"For about a month. While I'm here, Alex and I plan to settle Dad's estate and dispose of the business."

She could picture the sparkle that would have lighted his dark eyes. "I can't wait to see you again!"

As Sonya turned into the circular driveway, she thought of Dan and she as children looking for nonexistent treasures imagined to be hidden away by robbers along the banks of the Smoky Hill. She thought of Dan as she had last seen him over a year ago, when she'd wondered when the boy had changed so completely into a man — a very handsome man.

Sonya remained in the car for a while, weary from the long, monotonous miles of driving, filled with growing concern for Uncle Alex.

Before she'd reached the front steps of the house, Uncle Alex opened the door. "Look who's here," he drawled.

Sonya felt a sense of relief. In spite of his recent illness and the troubling events that had taken place in the long interval of her absence, Alex Brighton looked quite the same.

Uncle Alex couldn't possibly have married this woman! Through the huge front window of the Rathmell mansion, Sonya, a sinking sensation around her heart, watched Alex's bride, young enough to be his daughter, climb from the station wagon and move unhurriedly toward the house. She walked slowly, her exaggerated form giving her a voluptuous appearance. Silently Sonya compared her with Dan's mother — neat, fragile, righteous little Anna. Sonya could feel Alex's gaze on her. Of course he knew what she was thinking. He always did.

Her total disbelief at Uncle Alex's marrying only four months after Aunt Anna's death now changed to censure. The Brightons had suffered many shocks from Uncle Alex's activities, but none where his judgment about women was concerned.

Uncle Alex's wife was inside before she noticed any visitor. She wandered into the kitchen to set down a grocery sack and entered again, tossing a faded sun jacket on the buffet and reaching for a package of cigarettes.

Sonya glanced at Uncle Alex. The frosty, faded eyes, large with crinkled lines about them, always betrayed some contradiction, reading both laughter and meanness, sullenness and humor, suspicion and deep affection. Thin lips curved downward, deep furrows cut around them.

After an awkward silence, Sonya said, "I'm Alex's niece, Sonya Brighton. You must be Constance. Welcome to the clan."

"Call me Connie. You from Boston?"

"She runs Dexter Publications," Alex joked.

"I've heard Alex talk about you."

"So have I," Sonya answered, then to lighten the atmosphere, added, "Unfortunately."

Alex broke in again.

"This niece of mine is more like me than anyone on earth."

Sonya thought she detected some change in Connie's expression, an implication this was not what Connie considered good. Connie's gaze dropped to the canvas bag Sonya had placed beside the oak rocker. "You staying tonight?"

"She's staying as long as she can," Alex answered shortly. "Why don't you sell me that suitcase of yours? I'll give you a buck-fifty for it right now."

"I just paid ninety-nine-fifty."

"So, you got took. You'd better sell now

while you've got a buyer."

"He has to have someone to quibble with all the time," Connie observed coldly.

"I'll bet Sonya's hungry. Why don't you go open a couple of cans?"

Connie drew deeply on a cigarette and eyed him. He stared back.

"I hope you brought something home from town. All I could find here at noon was Meow Mix." He paused. "That blasted stray cat I took in eats better than I do. I think I'll start swapping meals with him."

Connie stuffed out the cigarette. "Shouldn't we wait for Emil and Sis?"

Alex answered a loud, definite, "No."

Sonya rose. "I love to cook. Let me help."

"No," Connie replied, then added in a definite way as if Sonya's assistance was the last thing she wanted, "You just stay in here and talk to him."

Connie ambled unconcernedly into the kitchen, and they could hear the clanging of kettles and the shuffle of silverware.

Alex turned to the source of the clatter.

"That woman sure makes a lot of noise!"

"So do you!" Connie yelled back at him from the other room.

"It used to be nice and peaceful-like around here."

Connie appeared at the doorway, knotting

11

a flowered apron behind her. She was silent as she smirked at Alex, then said to Sonya, "He wants to pick a fight now. No matter what I answer to that, there'll be an argument."

"It takes two to argue."

"But only one to start an argument, and you're always that one."

"Oh, forget I said anything. It never was peaceful here."

"Or anywhere around you," Connie added as she returned to the kitchen.

"I still have trouble with my hands." As Alex spoke, he rubbed the paralyzed fingers of his right hand. "But the feeling's coming back a little. It won't be long until I can work them as good as ever." He remained silent for a while, then, "How old are you? Twenty-two, twenty-three? When are you going to get married?"

Sonya, laughing as she always did at his abruptness, answered, "Never sounds like a good time."

"You don't have to get smart about it," Alex shot back teasingly. "I'm not so sold on marriage."

When he was seated, the paralytic straightness seemed to leave him entirely. His lean form now slumped in a relaxed, undisciplined way, hands folded across his stomach.

"Do you know Connie moved her sister and brother-in-law in with us? I don't know where they're at now, but they'll be here shortly. You can count on that."

Once again Sonya experienced a sinking sensation around her heart. She wished Alex wouldn't talk so loudly. Connie was certain to overhear. Not wanting to continue on the subject, Sonya said, "Maybe we can get Dad's estate settled while I'm here. I know we're going to take an awful loss on the furs, but we might just as well sell them. You haven't made any plans, have you?"

"No, I was waiting until you came back. I need to see to a lot of business. Have you noticed the 'FOR SALE' sign out here?"

Sonya felt jolted. She'd somehow over-looked the sign, had been too overwhelmed at the ruined look of the mansion. "I can't believe you actually intend to sell this place. You've always loved it here outside of town."

"Too much traffic. I'm getting weary of watching people crash and roll into my yard."

Sonya tried to put aside her shock at what she knew was his final decision, to sell out. She wanted very much to know his reason for selling — it must be a vital one, a last resort, but in spite of their years of confiding in one another, Sonya knew he wasn't likely to tell her.

"I've got a buyer already. But I've been waiting for you to get here to finalize the deal."

"Where are you going to move?"

Alex placed his hand on his knee and turned his head stiffly to look at her. "Down on Circle Street. It's not so nice a house, but it'll do. Besides, it's time I moved into town."

Gloomy silence settled over them. Then he sighed, and spoke in a quieter, slower tone.

"I can't begin to tell you what I went through after Anna died."

Sonya had at that time been working in London, had just been handed an assistant editorship at Dexter Publications. If she'd only known how bad things were for Uncle Alex, she would've abandoned her own plans and returned, but she hadn't known. She hadn't even been told he'd been struck with illness until last week, when she'd made this snap decision to see him.

Even though Alex was still in his sixties, the stroke had left him in bad need of assistance. He'd quickly accepted whatever aid was available. But why hadn't he turned to Dan, his stepson, who would have been willing to stand by him, instead of rushing

14

into an ill-thought-out remarriage?

Most of what Alex said, he didn't mean to be taken seriously, but his next words seemed more meaningful than humorous.

"Money grabbers," he said sourly. "Sometimes I feel as if I'm losing faith in humanity."

Now, with Connie so close by, wasn't the time to discuss Alex's very real problems. Sonya responded again, in a lighter vein. "Don't tell me you ever had faith in humanity."

"I did. But I finally learned. You can't trust anyone." Stillness filled the house, even out in the kitchen where Connie was preparing supper. Alex stared straight ahead. The space from his nose to his lip was wide and slightly protruding, adding bitterness to his mouth. "The best advice I can give you, Sonya, is this. Be always suspicious."

Connie's loud voice broke into the stillness. "He sure takes his own advice!"

"It's hard to keep up with the way things change," Sonya offered after a while.

"Yeah. Life takes much intestinal fortitude. And talking of courage, that's what it takes to eat Connie's cooking." Because he enjoyed maintaining a constant line of banter, he raised his voice so Connie couldn't miss hearing him. "Eating her

15

cooking is dangerous. Just like suicide!"

Connie, not short of quick retorts, stuck her head out of the kitchen entrance and made a face at him. "You're doing all right on my cooking. Getting fat and sassy."

Alex eyed her, a sardonic expression on his face.

"Sassy, maybe. But fat? I'm nothing but skin and bone."

Connie stepped into the front room, drying her hands on her apron. "He's always deviling me about my cooking. Someday I'm going to say, 'There's the stove, mister. You do the cooking'."

"Someday," Alex announced, "we might not have anything to cook. We'll be down there with those poor folks on Circle Street. They're not going to be able to bring in food like these neighbors do."

Connie's mouth tightened as she narrowed her eyes. "You'd better watch what you say, or Sonya will really think the neighbors have to feed us. You'll notice, Sonya, we hardly have any neighbors out here."

"What about LaVett?" Alex asked. "He's just across the field. Between him and the Salvation Army . . ."

Connie produced an exasperated woosh.

"Alex! I'll never understand him. We go

16

places and he pretends to lift billfolds, watches, or anything. I have to watch him all the time, so I can explain to everyone that he's just that way."

" 'That way'? You say that to everyone about me, and they'll think I'm insane."

"I wonder sometimes myself," Connie retorted quickly. "Wanting to move down on Circle Street."

"Don't start that again." The teasing vanished from Alex's voice. "That's settled."

Connie's bold gaze seemed to pierce him, but she didn't speak. Alex didn't look at her, nor at Sonya.

"What do you think of his selling this place?" Connie finally demanded.

Sonya remained silent, studying Connie. With her flawless skin and small, well-molded features, she did possess a certain attractiveness, yet the hardness of her eyes and the tense set of her thin lips revealed a capacity for scheming, for conniving. The affluent Rathmell Place with its vast areas of fertile land must look like very high stakes to her. Without doubt, Connie had plotted to turn Alex's situation to her advantage, to wrest the valuable property away from its natural heir, Anna's son, Dan.

17

"Speak up. Don't be shy. Alex isn't that fierce."

Alex got quickly to his feet. Sonya remembered when there had been a casual slump to his carriage, now he was forced to stand severely straight. "I told you not to start that again!"

Connie paid no attention. "I thought you might talk some sense into him, Sonya. He thinks so much of you, he might listen if you told him."

"I couldn't talk him out of anything." Sonya tried once again to regain their joking manner. "The Brightons are a stubborn lot."

"So I've found out. He told you, I suppose, what he's trying to make out of this place. Nothing compared to what it's worth! What's wrong with him? He's determined to sell this place for a song and live in a shack." Connie drew in her breath sharply. "That doesn't make any sense, does it? You'd better use your influence. I know you don't want to see that happen. Alex deserves it, but what about me?"

"Why don't you shut up!" Alex raised a hand as if to swipe her. "When you open your mouth, you bare your ugly soul!"

"You're just crazy to even think of selling out and moving down on that old street!

18

Don't you see? Nothing but trash lives down there."

"We ought to be right at home, then," Alex drawled.

"You just might be!"

Sonya turned and looked once again out of the window, toward gently rolling wheat fields beginning to turn yellow.

"Why don't you just ask Sonya what she thinks about it?" Connie demanded.

Sullenly, Alex sat back down on the leather couch. Sonya could tell by his brooding manner he would say no more but do exactly as he pleased.

"He never considers what anyone else wants." A calm, almost patient control now checked Connie's anger. "But tell him anyway, Sonya."

Sonya was musing on the issue. Connie had no doubt married Alex so she and her family would someday own the Rathmell place. She was surprised Alex hadn't protected himself from people like her.

"I'm sure Uncle Alex has his reasons for wanting to sell out."

"But you don't want to see him living down there. He's just going to end up losing his shirt!" As Connie spoke, she stepped closer, challenging Sonya to choose a side.

Sonya felt the sudden clash as their stares

met. Warning herself not to get involved, she made an effort to drive the opposition from her voice as she reminded Connie, "It is Alex's shirt."

CHAPTER 2

Two empty table settings had been placed around the huge, oak table in the kitchen, ready, no doubt, for Connie's sister and brother-in-law who would soon arrive. None for Dan, Sonya noticed

Doesn't Dan live here any longer?

She turned to ask Alex, "Where's Dan?"

Alex did not look back, just scowled, "Dan's moved into that little cabin across the field. Anna gave it to him before she died."

Sonya had known the moment she'd seen the condition of the house and the grounds that some major rift had occurred between her uncle and his stepson. Dan would never have allowed the Rathmell place to deteriorate the way it had in recent years if he could have prevented it.

She remembered dinners in the house, the fun and laughter. Alex and Dan had always gotten along very well. What could have happened to have separated them so completely?

"Let's eat," Alex said.

"Without Emil and Sis?"

Alex didn't answer Connie's question, just seated himself. The three quietly began the evening meal.

Connie's uneasy words soon broke into Sonya's thoughts. "Come on, Sis, Emil. Sit down and eat." Connie rose and added food to the dishes as she spoke.

The surprise Sonya had experienced upon meeting Alex's bride was minimal compared to the shock she now felt.

Emil, around Connie's age, possessed a towering height. His powerful body had a fixed, self-important straightness. He moved quickly around the vacant chair next to Alex, bypassing the waiting place setting, and seated himself on the other side of the table.

As Connie rearranged the dishes to suit him, Emil made no point of looking at Sonya, although Sonya knew he was well aware of her in a manner both distant and hostile.

"Sit down, Sis." Connie patted her sister's arm.

Alma's brown hair, short and tightly curled, lacked the luster and thickness of

Connie's, and unlike Connie, she had no claim to good looks. Despite Alma's slightly protruding teeth and broad, tapering cheeks, a slight resemblance still existed between the two, but only nebulous and only physical. Alma's manner was docile, her eyes possessed of a definite vagueness. Sonya found it hard to believe in the reality of a marriage between Alma and Emil, although she could most certainly picture him married to Connie.

"We have company tonight," Alma said with a joy unshared by the other two.

"Yes. Sonya, this is my sister, Alma, and her husband, Emil Steelman." Connie slipped back into the seat she had vacated. Emil and Alma's presence brought attention to the vacant chair between Uncle Alex and his wife.

Emil helped himself to the potatoes, heaping them high on his plate and pouring gravy over them by holding back the spoon and tipping the deep dish.

"Bring me the salt." The words were addressed to his wife.

Connie supplied him with the salt before her sister could do any more than comprehend the command. Sonya noticed how Emil's deepset eyes lingered on Connie with a glint of appreciation.

"Linnville hasn't changed much," Sonya forced herself to remark. "I had thought a lot of new businesses would have sprung up around the old Brighton Fur Company."

As she had expected, her words received no response. Sonya made several other attempts to talk to them, but each disintegrated into silence. Every time Sonya looked at Connie's sister, she would smile, but she, too remained quiet. The three of them huddled at their end of the table, each of them seemed to be lined up against Alex, who unpleasantly ignored them.

Sonya judged Emil to be the real source of Alex's trouble. And it was obvious being involved with this trio certainly was trouble! Alex, usually so worldly-wise, should have been prewarned.

How will he ever be able to extricate himself?

Alex was less content than she was to drift, he had never allowed problems to resolve themselves.

Before Sonya had finished eating, Alex rose, wiped his mouth with a napkin, and without a word, left. As soon as possible, Sonya excused herself and followed. For the first time she noticed how different the front room looked from her happy, childhood memories. The china cabinets crammed

24

with Anna's dishes, which she had prized so much, were gone. The tasteful antique furniture had been replaced by what was serviceable, but noticeably cheap, like the old leather couch near the small TV.

Not finding Uncle Alex, Sonya wandered outside. The Rathmell Place had been planned and built by the father of Anna's first husband, John T. Rathmell. First Alex had spoiled the majestic effect by building a garage beside it, and adjoining it, a shabby addition he proudly called his workshop. Here Sonya hoped to find him. She pushed open the shed door. A dim beam from a hanging bulb cast an eerie glow across tables stacked with tools, across walls lined with long-stored items of furniture. But he wasn't there.

She switched off the light as she left. The day had been hot, but the evening air felt cool and pleasant. Sonya listened to the quiet sounds, the locusts, the breeze against nearby branches. Only in Kansas could the skyline be so wide and clear, the moon so bright.

She strolled out into the field and paused to look toward the cabin where Dan was staying.

"Sonya."

Dan stood in the darkness beside the shed.

He'd been her childhood pal. After she'd left Kansas, she'd received more phone calls and letters from him than from Uncle Alex. In spite of this, Sonya found herself staring at him in startled silence as if he were some suspicious stranger.

"What?" he asked with a smile. "No, 'How are you, Dan?' No, 'Dan, I've missed you?' "

"Of course I've missed you," she managed.

The moonlight illuminated his straight nose, artfully shaped lips, alert dark eyes. The glow made him look gentle and noble, a glorious merging of the best of Anna and John Rathmell.

"Let's drive to Linnville this evening," he suggested. "We could go to Malroy's and dance a little. You still like pizza, don't you?"

Sonya found herself hesitating.

"I think I should stay here tonight, Dan."

She went on, feeling Dan's gaze growing solemn as she attempted to explain. "Alex seems . . . very upset."

A muscle moved in Dan's jaw, but he made no comment.

To break the oppressive stillness, Sonya asked, her voice sounding strangely formal to her, "How have you been? Are you still in law school?"

"Yes. I have one more year before I can

take the bar exams. I've kept Dad's old office and hope to open it again some day." Dan stopped speaking suddenly, and his old, easy smile returned, and with it a glint of admiration. "But look at you, already the editor of an international magazine."

"Not so wonderful as it sounds," Sonya replied. "This is my first time off in over a year. I find I never get away from the pressure, from the work."

Sonya went on, feeling as if she were talking just for the sake of filling the silence, sidestepping the subjects important to her. "Traveling across country gave me the idea of doing a series of articles about old homes, like this one."

"Like this one was," Dan corrected. "I've got some photographs of the way it used to look, if that will be of any help. We can drive over to Talbert, too, and take pictures of the Talbert Mansion."

The helpfulness, that's what she remembered most about Dan, the quality that would have compelled him to take on Uncle Alex's problems as if they were his own.

They began walking side by side back toward the house.

"It's hard to believe that Uncle Alex really intends to sell this place."

As Sonya spoke, she cast Dan a quick,

sideways glance, but could read no emotion in his features. She'd expected to see anger or deep resentment. After all, everyone expected that by rights his parents' home would some day pass to him.

Dan's stony silence increased her uneasiness, caused her to say defensively, "Maintaining property like this is a big task. Uncle Alex has been in no condition to see to it."

"I could have done that for him."

Sonya stopped walking.

"Please tell me, Dan. What's happened between Alex and you?"

Dan gazed at her grimly, and she knew that, like Alex, he was going to keep whatever trouble existed between them to himself. "It's very involved, Sonya — everything is."

"Because of Alex's marriage? Because of Emil Steelman?"

"I don't know just what's going on here. If I did, I'd tell you."

They had reached the porch. Dan, trying to claim their old easy rapport, smiled, and said, "I know you're an early riser. Why don't we meet tomorrow morning and look over the farm together?"

Sonya thought of them as free and happy children, roaming across the vast land, swimming in the pond, exploring the banks of the river.

"An early morning walk, I'd like that."

The smile remained on Dan's face. The moonlight made him fascinatingly handsome.

"Then don't forget. Seven."

Sonya almost called him back to tell him she'd changed her mind, but Dan was already out of sight behind the shed. Why did she have to be torn between Dan and her uncle? Yet she was, and she knew that her seeing Dan was going to make matters worse instead of better, was likely to serve as a wedge that would drive them even further apart. Sonya entered the house feeling as if her meeting with Dan tomorrow would surely end in disaster.

Uncle Alex sat on the cot in the front room, his dour features shadowy in the dim light. His presence startled her.

"You want to hear about money-grabbers?" he asked.

For an instant, she felt greatly disturbed. She read in his face a lingering anger, as if he knew that Dan had just left. She seated herself stiffly in the rocker across from him and managed to say lightly, "Why not. You know that's my favorite subject."

"Jody called me from California."

"Is she still there?" Sonya asked, a little relieved. "Last I heard she was in Vegas."

Sonya's cousin, Jody, lived an unpredictable life. After Dad and Jody's parents had been killed in a car accident, Jody had lost no time taking to the road.

Alex didn't answer her question, but had his opinions about Jody.

"Jody didn't have time to attend Anna's funeral, but she wanted to come afterwards. To see what she could get," he added.

Sonya found it hard to believe that besides Alex, Jody and she were the last of the Brightons. Sonya had always liked her even though she found Jody's free, dutyless life-style hard to accept. Not a cousin to be proud of — but Alex hadn't assessed Jody quite correctly. She was more reckless and unthinking than greedy or grasping.

"Did Jody ever show up?"

"She called from Fresno for me to wire her money," Alex said. "I didn't, and that's the last I heard from her. With any luck, it'll stay the last I'll hear from her."

Sonya smiled and, to encourage him to keep up his familiar, crusty humor, observed, "One money-grabber eliminated."

He didn't return her lightness. "One bigger one very much present — Dan Rathmell!"

Immediately, her visions of a joyous reunion with the two people she loved most totally faded. Oppressive silence hung between them as Alex waited for her to respond.

"Dan never was concerned with . . . what other people concern themselves with." The sentence sounded as awkward as she felt.

Alex's frosty eyes locked on hers. "Don't you know that someone came into my house right after Anna's funeral and stole everything they could get their hands on?"

Sonya was fast growing accustomed to the sinking feeling around her heart. She didn't manage a verbal answer, only a shake of her head.

"I was robbed while I was flat on my back with that stroke."

He seemed to be accusing Dan, but that couldn't be. Alex would know Dan wouldn't steal.

"Who do you think did it? Did the sheriff find any clues?"

"The sheriff wouldn't be able to find his own footprints."

Sonya's thoughts flitted at once to Emil Steelman.

"You surely have some idea."

The corners of Alex's mouth drooped.

31

"Not that I want to discuss. But I think whoever robbed me did it for pure spite."

"What did the thief take?"

"You know how Anna loved jewelry. All of that's gone — her diamonds, rubies, pearls. Even that big Black Hills gold ring you gave her, the one with the horseshoe. I've never seen another one like it. Whoever broke in took antiques, quilts and fancy work, silver and dishes. He probably would have carted off the refrigerator if he could have carried it."

"Why didn't you call me?"

"You have your own problems. Besides, what could you do? I pressured the police, but they didn't get anywhere."

"Wasn't Dan living here then?"

Alex's eyes iced over a little more at her mention of Dan.

"No. He moved down to the cabin before Anna died."

Sonya studied him, knowing he had no intention of talking over with her what he knew or suspected. She'd always admired his fierce independence, although right now it was standing between her and the truth.

Alex must believe that after Dan's mother died, Dan had intruded into his house and stolen everything he wanted, valuables Anna had doubtlessly trusted Alex to someday pass on to him.

Sonya continued her study of Alex. His life had been filled with many battles. In the silence Sonya recalled the trouble that had often erupted between her father and him. It had centered for the most part around that foolish venture, their partnership in Brighton Furs. The fur business had been completely unsuited to Alex, even though it had been his own idea, one he had gotten during a summer spent in Alaska.

At one time, the business had been thriving, but in recent years the market had changed for the worse. Sonya thought of the great stock of expensive furs — ermine, mink, and silver fox, that they must now sell; of the remains of the business needing to be discontinued. To overcome the oppressive stillness, Sonya finally made a suggestion.

"Let's go to the warehouse tomorrow. We can decide what to do with . . ."

Sonya was interrupted by Connie's sister entering from the kitchen. Alma moved to Sonya's chair, smiling and saying, "It's nice to have company."

"It's good to be here."

Immediately Alex rose. "I've sold a lot of the furniture that used to be upstairs. I told them to bring in one of the beds from the shed and set it up in a spare room, but they didn't."

He paused. "I'll see to it tomorrow. Tonight, you can sleep here on the couch."

He swung abruptly to Alma. "Sonya's tired. You go on upstairs and leave her alone."

Alma, shrinking at his words, scrambled toward the stairway. Alex soon walked out, too, leaving Sonya immersed in the chilling emptiness of the front room.

For many hours, twisting and turning on the hard, leather couch, she tried to stop the intruding visions of Dan.

Dan appearing from the shadows of the shed, Dan lurking outside the house, waiting for the opportunity to rob the man who'd raised him, the strong man rendered helpless by illness.

Why, when she could not in her heart believe it possible, did those images persist and cause a chill to settle deep into her heart?

Chapter 3

From the couch in the front room, Sonya could hear Alex banging around in the kitchen. He'd risen before sunrise and had made excessive noise, sounds so loud they couldn't be muffled by her pillow. She now heard footsteps coming closer. A quiet moment. Then, "Get up!"

Sonya didn't stir.

"Anyone who sleeps later than I do is lazy!"

"I don't get up before breakfast," Sonya replied, pulling the blanket up over her head.

"I had an old dog that used to sleep most of the day. I figured he was worthless, so I shot him."

Sonya removed the cover.

"Don't shoot! I'll get up!"

She dressed in the bathroom at the top of the stairs. The image in the mirror didn't indicate evidence of the long, sleepless night. Her gray eyes looked bright and clear, her charcoal hair springy and shiny. Six o'clock — in one hour she was to meet Dan. Reservations loomed like heavy clouds. Because Uncle Alex and Dan weren't getting along, she sincerely wished she'd not made plans to meet him.

Alex, standing near the kitchen stove, poured hotcake batter onto the sputtering griddle. The familiar sight pleased her, brought back memories of her childhood, where, left free in the kitchen, Alex, Dan, and she had made messes that Anna had complained about for days.

She watched the laborious movement of his stiff fingers. "It's wonderful," she said, "the way you're recovering from that stroke."

"If it wasn't for these . . ." he gazed with distaste at his hands, ". . . I'd be as good as new. It's an ordeal to do even ordinary things, like gripping a spoon. The doctor says I ought to have more patience. He says everything's coming along fine. That's the natural thing for him to say, though. The only time he looks at my hands with any interest is when there's money in them."

Sonya accepted the cup of coffee Alex supplied and seated herself at the table. She drank her coffee black and didn't know why she kept stirring it. "How did you ever meet Connie?"

If he thought the question abrupt or none of her business, his quick answer didn't reveal it.

"You know Anna was never very strong. Connie and Alma used to do the laundry for us and clean house. I stayed alone those three months after Anna died during the winter. Connie got to telling me I needed someone to stay here and do the cooking, so finally I hired her as house-keeper." Generally Alex avoided looking at people when he talked — now his pale eyes trans-fixed hers. "Then people got to talking. Connie kept worrying about what they were saying. I told her to tell them to mind their own business, but you know women. A month later we were married."

Sonya dropped her gaze from his intent eyes. "How long have her sister and Emil Steelman been here?"

"Connie lost no time moving them in. At first, I didn't care. I've got plenty of room."

"At first?"

"Connie's sister is a pest, but for the most part she stays out of my way. That's more than I can say for Emil. He treats Alma like dirt, but he'll do anything for Connie."

"Last night he seemed rather distant."

"The more distant he is, the better. Trouble is, he isn't distant enough."

"What does he do?"

"You mean, does he work?" Alex laughed. "Not that I know of. He's an over-aged wrestler. Used to call himself Mr. Satan."

Sonya smiled. "That seems to fit."

At that moment, Connie entered the room. She must have overhead Sonya's comment, but she didn't react to it. She turned the fire up under the sausage and began rearranging it with the spatula.

Sonya glanced at Alex, who merely finished his coffee, pushed back his chair, and strode from the kitchen. Once in the front room, he turned on the radio, and the blare of trumpets lambasted the house.

Connie went about her business, breaking an egg into the skillet, spreading hot grease over it. She worked with rushless ease. Sonya noticed the shiny black hair clipped on either side with pins. She was clad in an old flannel robe and wore a pair of Alex's carpet slippers. Still she was able to hold a person's gaze.

Connie scooped the eggs and sausage onto her plate and slipped languidly into the chair Alex had vacated.

"I can't stand that music," she said. "He's turned that on just to aggravate me."

Irascibly she pushed the plate away from her. She remained motionless for a moment, then clamped a hand across her forehead and burst out, "Turn that damn thing down!"

Instantly, Alex yelled back.

"If you don't like it, go somewhere else!"

"That's what I should have done a long time ago!"

Sonya's gaze strayed to the wall clock — almost seven. Dan would be waiting. She should go out and talk to him, tell him she couldn't see him this morning, and drive with Alex to the warehouse.

As soon as possible, she left the kitchen, turning down the volume of the radio as she passed it. In the mirror over the buffet, she saw a reflection of the empty front room, all the more vacant because she'd expected to see Uncle Alex seated on the leather couch.

One thing she wanted to avoid at all costs was any confrontation between Dan and her uncle. She took the opportunity Alex's absence offered and hurried outside. As she walked down the steps, she thought of Dan and how handsome he'd looked in the moonlight.

The cool morning air refreshed her. A farmer in a pickup, slowing for the curb, waved to her. She increased the speed of her steps, feeling the excitement of seeing Dan again.

His voice came from behind her. He must have been inside Alex's workshop, or she would have noticed him as she passed. Had Alex been out here this morning and left the shed unlocked, or did Dan have a key to it?

Dan's eyes, almost black in the daylight, glowed with the satisfaction of seeing her. She felt herself responding to the power of his personality, and temporarily she put aside her regret at not being able to spend any time with him this morning.

Dan caught her hand, and they started out across the field. Soon he bent and snipped a blade of yellowing wheat, placing it between his lips.

"You are becoming a farmer," Sonya said.

"Only an appreciator of beauty." He stopped walking to look at her. "The wheat is beautiful and so are you."

Flattery, but pleasing none the less. She felt a warmth rise to her face. Once again, she postponed her message.

"Do you remember where we used to swim?"

Sonya's gaze lifted toward the sharp rise of land across the field to the south. In the draw just beyond it, cottonwoods grew in abundance, encircling a large expanse of deep, muddy water. There, under Anna's supervision, Dan had tossed his stones and launched his paper boats, and they had swum.

"The pond is deeper this year because of all the rain," he said. "It's become my private swimming pool."

His dark eyes sparkled in a way that had always intrigued her. "But I'd share it with you. Why not this afternoon?"

"I'm afraid . . ." Sonya's voice drifted off.

"Of frogs and water bugs," he finished. "I'll let you knight me as your protector."

She laughed. "A rain check," she answered. "We'll have to walk another time, too. This morning Alex and I have business in Linnville."

"You can't let business take up all of your time. When are you free?"

She noted Dan's reaction to her silence and sensed overpowering sadness looming.

"The way things are between Uncle Alex and you, our seeing each other right now is probably not a good idea."

Not wanting to watch Dan's joy over their reunion change to grimness, Sonya quickly turned away. She began walking back toward the house.

41

Dan, lagging behind her a little, followed.

"I'm not going to allow anyone or anything to stop me from seeing you," he asserted. "I've waited a long time for you to come back."

"We'll get together later. Right now, Alex needs my help."

"I hope you have better luck helping him than I've had."

"We could see him through this trouble if we worked together. We must find some way to repair this breach between you two."

"I've tried. Frankly, I don't think it can be repaired."

"You used to get along so well. Can't you at least give me a clue to what happened?"

He shook his head. Not continuing on the subject, not supplying her with any reasons for his estrangement with Alex, Dan said, "We can't let what's happened between Alex and me separate us."

Catching her arm, he gazed at her earnestly. "If you don't have time this morning, then meet me this afternoon. I'll be at the pond at two."

Sonya felt her opposition weakening. She was almost ready to agree, when a belligerent voice sounded from the shed.

"I told you not to come around this house."

Alex stepped from the entrance, pale eyes chilled. The severely erect way he stood added to his menacing appearance.

Dan swung around to face him.

The two men stared at each other. Sonya's heart pounded as she read the deep anger on their faces, anger that might at any moment explode into open warfare.

Knowing Dan wouldn't be the one to instigate further trouble, Sonya addressed her plea to her uncle. "Alex, let's just go back to the house."

Alex's gaze stayed on Dan. "You stay away from Sonya," he said acidly.

"Sonya can choose her own company."

Dan, although very controlled, his voice strangely quiet, seemed every bit as deadly as her uncle.

Alex stepped forward ominously.

"You're not going to see her. Not while I'm able to prevent it."

"Alex," Sonya interceded. "Dan and I grew up together. You're not being fair."

"As fair as he is."

The lines in Alex's face deepened as he addressed himself to Dan again. "You have some nerve, stepping foot on my property again. You know you're not welcome here any longer."

Dan, instead of leaving, took a step closer

to Alex. Open conflict, just what Sonya had wanted so desperately to prevent. Almost in panic, she groped for words that would deter the clash threatening to break between them. The only word that came to her was 'Anna'.

"Anna loved you both. Can't you possibly get along for her sake, for her memory?"

Dan's expression of coldness, a look she'd never before seen in him, softened a little at the mention of his mother's name. Without a word, he gazed at Sonya, then as if he didn't want to force her to choose between opposing loyalties, he turned on his heel and strode away.

Sonya wanted to rush after him, to ease the hurt she knew he was feeling. She forced herself to stay beside Uncle Alex.

Alex glared after Dan.

"I didn't want to tell you, but I guess I'll have to. Dan was the one who robbed me."

"Oh, no! Dan would never do that!"

"I didn't want to believe it either, Sonya, but I've got solid proof."

Alex didn't look at her, still stared after Dan as he spoke. In spite of his usual brusqueness which she knew masked his vulnerability, his voice had betrayed a deep sense of pain over what he believed was Dan's betrayal.

"It couldn't have been Dan. How could you even think that it was him?"

"A few days after the robbery, my neighbor, LaVett, and I took a little look around Dan's cabin. Dan had disposed of everything else, except for some of Anna's jewelry that he'd placed in a folder in the bottom drawer of his desk."

It would take more than that to convince Sonya Dan was a thief.

"Anyone could have planted those items there expecting the police to find them."

"The anyone you're talking about would have no reason to believe Dan's cabin was going to be searched."

Sonya needed to know more, and eyed the landscape somberly as though she could find answers hidden in the trees.

"Did you discuss what you found with the sheriff? Did you sign —"

"He is Anna's son," Alex interrupted bitterly.

Sonya drew in her breath. "Are you positive the jewels belonged to Anna?"

"I couldn't be wrong about the ring. It was the Black Hills gold horseshoe you sent to Anna when you were in South Dakota. Dan would have wanted it for sentimental reasons, because Anna was so delighted when you gave it to her." Alex's tone lowered, became even more certain. "If some-one was trying to frame Dan, he'd have hidden one of Anna's valuable diamond pieces in his house. That would have been much more incriminating."

Alex's convincing argument left Sonya feeling half-stunned. "That doesn't mean Dan's guilty. Whoever placed the ring in his cabin just used one you would be certain to recognize."

Her words, adamant though they were, couldn't wipe out the accusing silence that followed.

"I'm fed up with the whole lot of them," Alex said finally. "You're the only person I know that I can trust. Just like my own daughter. I'm going to give you a father's advice. Stay away from Dan Rathmell!"

CHAPTER 4

Uncle Alex threw open the first door along the dark hallway. "A spooky-looking place to put a guest," he said. "Maybe you should draw those drapes."

Sonya stepped over to the window and obliged.

In days long past, this grand, master bedroom had been occupied by Anna and John T. Rathmell, whose picture still hung above the fireplace. The sudden thrust of light into the room revealed the threadbare trails across the wine-colored Oriental rug and pointed out years of neglect. An unpleasant odor of mildew hung in the air.

"I asked Connie to have this cleaned out, but I knew she wouldn't. I'll help you knock down the cobwebs. The rest is up to you. It sure is gloomy though. The couch is still downstairs, if you don't like it here."

Of the once fabulous furnishings, only an ancient desk and chair, too ponderous and bulky to remove, remained. An old iron bed taken from the shed had been set up where Anna's walnut one, with headboard that had towered to the ceiling, had once set.

"Kind of bare," Alex observed.

"This will be fine."

Alex took a step closer to the fireplace. "Why Anna loved John Rathmell is beyond me," he said.

Sonya followed Alex's frosty gaze toward the picture. The painted face of John T. Rathmell bore a startling resemblance to Dan's, except for a certain haughtiness evident by the lift of his chin and the slight arch of dark brow. The faint smile on lips, much fuller than Dan's, made Sonya feel slightly uncomfortable.

"A snob and a scoundrel!" Alex's words boomed theatricality. He added, with the humor he always used as a shield, "The scoundrel part of it, Dan intends to carry on."

Alex walked to the door and not looking back, said a little wearily, "I don't feel like going to the warehouse today."

After he left, Sonya wandered back to the huge, circular window. Beyond the sloping roof of the porch, she could see the winding highway and hear the sound of early-morning traffic.

The deterioration of eves and roof, the condition of Anna's room, made Sonya realize that this was the ending of an era — the Rathmell Place would never again hold a position of honor in the community, would never again be filled with laughter and parties and important guests.

Saddened, she made the bed, began cleaning the room, and arranging her clothes in the huge closet. She finally started back downstairs, hoping that Uncle Alex had changed his mind about not going to the warehouse.

Halfway down the stairs, voices from the front room drifted to her. Emil Steelman, demanding.

"We need that money now. It'll make all the difference."

"Grandma gave the money to me. Only for me, so I'd always have something." Alma's voice, deeply fearful but tinged with stubbornness. She was taking a firm stand against her husband.

"What kind of security is six thousand dollars these days? I put up with your hanging on to it when I wanted to start that garage, but now things are different. Connie needs this money." Emil's voice grew harsher, more strident. "You've always put Connie's wishes above everyone else's. I don't know why you're so bent now on just thinking of yourself."

"Grandma gave the money to me," Alma repeated. "I promised Grandma."

Sonya drew a deep breath and opened the door. Emil immediately swung around to face her. The brutish set of his neck on enormous shoulders, and his secretive, shaded eyes, gave her a moment of fright.

"Have you seen Alex?" Sonya directed her question to Alma.

Alma, as if lost in her own despondent thoughts, didn't at first reply. When she did speak, she asked a question of her own.

"Do you want Alex to sell this house? Connie says you do. She says that's why you came back here."

"Connie's wrong. I came back here most of all to see Uncle Alex."

Emil gave a contemptuous snort. "You came too late," he said. "Brighton needs a guardian, has for a long time."

Sonya met Emil's challenge. "Uncle Alex is quite capable of looking after his own affairs."

Emil pushed aside the drape and stared outside in scornful silence. His eyes followed the movement of someone crossing the yard.

In a few seconds, Connie pushed through

the door.

"Alex knew I wanted to use the car this morning, so what does he do? He drives right off. He's headed out toward the barn of all places." She paused, then added in an exasperated way, "If the doctor told him to work, he'd probably spend his life in bed."

Sonya, feeling unable to remain in the house with them any longer, quickly went outside. If she were able to find Uncle Alex, maybe he'd change his mind about going to the warehouse.

As a child, in awe of the rich, thick furs, she used to trail along to the store with Dad. She hadn't seen the warehouse, the over-flowing inventory, for over a year. They should have settled the business right after Dad had died, but neither Alex nor she at that time had any heart to do so. Now it had grown into a tedious and heavy burden, one among many.

The barn was located just beyond Dan's cabin. Perhaps she could catch up with Uncle Alex there. Even if she didn't, the walk would do her good, would help clear her mind.

She chose to follow the ridgeline where she would be able to glimpse the river flowing through town, where far in the distance she would be able to see the cluster of houses and the gray water tower of Linn-ville.

As she cut across the wheat field, sunlight bore down upon her, the heat intense against her bare arms. Sonya began to feel smothered by the still, oppressive air and by her own thoughts. Alex was dealing with a very tough opportunist in Emil. Considering Alex's health, he might be up against more than he could handle.

The thought left her fearful. Even if Dan, Alex, and she all worked together — which they weren't doing — they'd have trouble freeing Alex from those plotting people she had left back at his house.

Of course, Alex had some plan of his own in mind. He always did. Selling this property, or making it look as if he intended to sell out, must be a part of it. But how could Sonya help him if he continued to stubbornly work alone?

Feeling even more distraught than she had back at the house, Sonya reached the edge of the field and started up the steep slope. Below, the pond — Dan's pond — looked cool and inviting. She hesitated a moment, then, on impulse began winding her way through thick trees and sumac stocks until she reached the pool's edge.

She knelt and allowed her hand to stir

through the tepid water. Then she lifted her gaze to locate the huge oak tree with the thick limb stretching so far across the pond. She remembered the many times Dan had climbed out on it to dive. The image of Dan became so vivid she could almost hear the splash of his hard body against water.

The peaceful quietness was broken by a faint sound, like a furtive step on crackling twigs. She straightened up, her gaze skirting through the thickness of branches.

She remained immobile for a while, watching, listening, hoping for Dan to materialize and quiet her growing sense of fear.

Images of the faces of the three conspirators she'd left in Alex's house blotted out thoughts of Dan. She knew they considered her sudden arrival here as a personal threat to them. She could visualize Emil stalking her, hiding back there in the thick tangle of trees and foliage.

She lost no time, feet sliding against lose rocks and dirt, hurrying back up the steep slope. Once there, not feeling quite so defenseless, she remained a while, surveying the entire area of the pond. Sonya detected no movement below her. She knew she was edgy, that imagination could be intruding into reality.

She began walking along the ridgeline

again. She could see Dan's cabin. The oaks and cottonwoods so abundant in the draw didn't encroach into the level land around the small, white house. That, alone, made it look stark and solitary.

Sonya glimpsed no sign of activity. She was disappointed, for she suddenly very much wanted to talk to Dan.

The sprawling old barn on the far edge of Brighton land, like the house itself, showed an air of neglect. Beneath the faded red paint, she could see that the exposed boards were rotting and beginning to crumble. More anxious than ever to locate Alex, Sonya hurried forward, noticing that a battered pickup was backed into the open doorway.

She could see someone inside the barn, clad in dusty denim. She watched the ease with which he carried a heavy bale of hay, tossing it high upon the stack lining the wall. As he started back to the truck, sunlight fell across his coppery skin, lighting large blue eyes, which widened when his gaze met hers. A hand rose to sweep back very straight hair, the exact color of the hay he stacked.

"I didn't mean to startle you," she said. "I'm looking for Alex."

"He just left."

"Did he say where he was headed?"

"Probably to Linnville. He generally stops whenever he sees me here, but today he didn't stay long." The tall, muscular man drew closer, and she smelled the scent of straw and earth clinging to him.

"I know who you are." The smile made him look very young and carefree. "Sonya Brighton. Alex is always talking about you."

His outstretched hand, at this late point in their meeting, seemed awkward, but his tight grip was warm and friendly. "I'm Melvin LaVett. Your uncle's my best friend. I borrow everything from him, even his barn."

"You must live close by."

"About a year ago, I moved into the old Bailey place. I've been fixing it up," he added.

Melvin LaVett had about him a certain earnestness she liked. She returned his smile.

"I'm glad you're here," he said. "Alex has had quite a time, losing his wife and being hit with that stroke."

Sonya met the level gaze of his very blue eyes. "Alex loved Anna so much. I was surprised when I heard he had remarried."

" 'Marry in haste . . .' " Melvin started, but his voice trailed off.

Sonya took this opportunity to press him for information.

"Do you know anything about Connie or the Steelmans?"

"Small-town rumors, that's all."

Sonya persisted. "Concerning what?"

Melvin avoided looking at her as he spoke.

"There's people out there," he said, "who are constantly looking for . . . easy prey."

Sonya hadn't expected him to be quite so forthright. She found herself at a momentary loss for words.

"I'm not saying that's what happened here," he immediately qualified. "You see, I don't really know them that well. Connie, herself, doesn't seem all that bad, but I can't say the same for Emil Steelman."

When Sonya didn't reply, he went on. "I tried to warn Alex. I told him he must look very wealthy to them, but in a way I couldn't blame him for marrying Connie. He was in such bad need of help."

"He had Dan here."

Melvin seemed on the verge of confiding more, but perhaps as if he thought he'd said too much already, he changed the subject.

"Are you going to be here long?"

"I'm not sure yet. Alex has been talking of selling out. Has he mentioned it to you?"

"I don't think he'll actually go through

56

with any sale," Melvin replied. "This place is too much a part of him."

"I hope you're right." Sonya turned to leave. "We'll probably be seeing each other again."

"Sonya, I'll be through here in a minute. I can give you a lift back across the field."

"Thanks, but I'm enjoying the walk. If you run across Alex again, tell him I'm looking for him."

Melvin LaVett, not seeming anxious to get back to work, remained in the doorway of the barn. She could sense his stare following her as she crossed the field. Meeting him gave her some consolation. Uncle Alex had at least one loyal friend and supporter besides herself.

Alex's station wagon was angled in front of the porch as if it had been parked in haste by someone who intended to leave again.

As Sonya entered the front room, Emil was saying to Alex, who stood near the kitchen door, "I'm just thinking of what's best for you."

"And I want only what's best for you," Alex answered curtly.

Alma, swaying back and forth in the rocker, smiled, as if knowing both of them had meant exactly what they said.

Even though it appeared to remain intent

on Alex, Emil's gaze slyly, calculatingly, took in Sonya's arrival. "Property's a good investment," he stated in a slow, sinister way. "Money gets away."

"I'll have to remember that."

"I'd say this place is worth far over a million," Emil spoke again. "The way land and property has been selling here."

"Don't try to make my decisions."

"Alex," Sonya cut in. "Why don't we go into Linnville now?"

"Not now, Sonya. I'm going to rest for a while." He walked out.

"He's mad," said Alma mournfully the moment he'd gone. "He's always mad at us."

"Oh, be quiet," Emil growled.

Sonya, feeling an intense need to get away from them again, hurried up the stairs.

Uncle Alex didn't appear for the evening meal. Sonya ate quickly and returned to her room, which had grown increasing gloomy with approaching darkness.

She sank down at the desk and attempted to write about the house, trying to recall how it had looked to her as a child. The wondrous antiques, the grand chandeliers, the great oil paintings — had Alex been forced to sell all of them to pay the bills?

Being seated at John T. Rathmell's marred, walnut desk drew her thoughts toward Dan's father, and she wondered what he'd been like, what had caused his father before him to settle in this small, Kansas town, to build such a mansion on an isolated prairie. She looked at his portrait, hanging over the fireplace. For some reason Alex had allowed it to remain. In the dim light, John T. Rathmell's features really did bear an uncanny likeness to Dan's. The familiar, handsome face gazing down at her made her feel more and more uncomfortable, as if Dan, too, had been plotting against Uncle Alex.

She quickly brushed aside the notion. She needed to see Dan. A talk with him would be certain to help to calm her fears and doubts. How was she ever going to accomplish the impossible, to find some way to reconcile the two most important people in her life?

Fully dressed, wide awake, Sonya lay across the bed trying to drive away fear and tenseness. She couldn't stop the bombarding thoughts.

She'd not known until she'd seen the condition of the property that her uncle was having money worries. The house and land might already be mortgaged, financial problems might be forcing a sale. Or could it be that Alex was just trying to outmaneuver Connie . . . or Dan?

Poor Alex, he was under attack from every side. Grief and great pressure topped with unexpected illness had prompted his sudden marriage to Connie. Melvin LaVett might be right in thinking Alex was selling out as a means of freeing himself from a bad decision.

Alex wouldn't need Connie's signature in order to finalize the sale, for after Anna died the deed would be in his name alone. Alex would be aware of the fact that Connie had married him so she could someday own the Rathmell Place. What he would be uncertain about was just how far Connie and her henchman, Emil, were going to go to keep the property from slipping away from them.

Hours later, Sonya fell into a light, troubled sleep. She was jarred awake by a sharp pounding on the door. Sitting up abruptly, startled because the room was pitch black, she called, "Who's there?"

Someone pushed open the door. A brilliant light glared, causing her to shield her eyes, and for a moment she couldn't recognize the person who had entered her room.

Uncle Alex stood above her, his form tense and straight.

"The warehouse!" he said brusquely. "It's caught on fire!"

CHAPTER 5

Alex swung the station wagon around, and it roared toward the highway. He didn't slow for the curve and stepped down harder on the gas as the road straightened to Linnville. An ominous reddish glow could be seen even from this distance.

"It must be a bad one," Alex said acidly. "It'll probably take everything."

The Brighton Fur building, isolated except for the wheat elevator beside it, dominated the south side of Linnville, just inside the city limits. Black smoke hovered threateningly over the bare fields and encroached across the highway.

Alex, ignoring the directions of a fireman, drove between the close-spaced, orange barriers and pulled to a stop behind the fire trucks. Without a word, he disappeared into the shifting crowd.

Flames, enclosing the warehouse, leaped angrily into darkness. Everywhere firemen scurried, dragging hoses and shouting. Streams of water made little progress against the solid mass of fire.

Nothing here would be salvaged. Sonya observed the destruction sadly, as she would have watched the funeral of an old friend. Big and sturdy, an important part of her past, the warehouse had seemed to her a landmark which would always be around, shielded from time, change, or ruin.

Not cheered by the fact that Alex and she would no longer have to struggle with the settlement of Dad's estate, Sonya had been prepared to take a loss on the sale of the warehouse and the stock. Alex and she expected to receive little more out of the final close-out than what was required to meet the debts still owed by the business. Not the case now — insurance money would supply them with a more than substantial gain. Uncle Alex would consider this fire a fortunate and timely streak of luck.

But was it luck? Something was definitely wrong with the way Uncle Alex was acting. He didn't seem startled enough — almost as if he'd known about the devastation of the building in advance. The roaring flames began to have the same weakening effect on Sonya that they had on the huge structure. She leaned for support against the open door of the car. Surely Alex would have nothing to do with arson, no matter how badly he might need cash.

If only Uncle Alex had stayed beside her, some reassuring word or action might have been able to combat her growing doubts. The brilliant flames, lapping high into the darkness, increased her fear. She drew in her breath as the huge sign 'Brighton Furs' fell, crashing into the inferno. Thousands and thousands of dollars worth of furs had already been transformed into ashes and charred rubble.

Sonya began winding her way through the spectators, searching for Uncle Alex. Of course, in such a small town everyone would be certain to recognize her. Eyes focused on her, moved in silent communication to one another as she passed. She could sense their accusations. The intense heat made her feel feverish. Oppressive smoke filled her lungs so she could hardly breathe. She faltered, struggling with an urge to cry.

A strong, guiding hand caught her arm and steered her away from the smoke and the people. Dan's white shirt, discolored by ashes, appeared as ruffled and messed as his hair. A black smudge darkened the broad line of his jaw.

"Do you know what they're saying?" he

asked, angrily.

Dan's outraged tone added to her misery. She couldn't bring herself to answer, only to give a slight shake of her head.

"Sonya." His voice softened. His eyes became gentle, reminding her of Anna's, and he lifted a hand in an attempt to smooth her disheveled hair. Sonya fought a desire to move into the safety and protection of his arms.

"The sheriff got a call about ten-fifteen. The caller said he saw someone inside the warehouse, a robber, he thought. When the sheriff checked, he found all doors and windows locked. A short time later the place exploded in flames."

Sonya tensed as she asked the inevitable question.

"Do they think it was deliberately set?"

Dan paced away from her a few steps. Firelight flickered across his face, highlighting his finely-chiseled features.

"You can be sure the fire will be investigated." He turned back to her. "They think Alex hired someone to burn this place in order to collect insurance."

"That might be hard to prove, especially since it couldn't happen — Alex wouldn't do anything like that."

"They have a witness, Sonya. He might be

able to identify whoever entered the warehouse tonight."

"Who's the witness?"

"Tom Bradley. He was driving back to his
farm."

She shrugged hopelessly.

"I hope he did recognize someone. Because we didn't have anything to do with
it."

"I know you didn't, Sonya."

Their silence left only the crackling sounds
of the fire. The building's office, once so
impressive with its smart glass front, could
no longer be identified. Sonya shuddered,
spoke again as she watched.

"Connie's so opposed to Alex's selling the
farm. Do you think Emil might have done
this so Alex would have ready cash and want
to keep the place?"

"We can only guess at what's happened,"
Dan replied.

Sonya cast a guarded glance toward him.
Dan's dark eyes, reflecting crimson light,
locked on the flames, hurled toward them
by a strong gust of wind. The burning
intensity of his expression seemed a match
for the fire.

Thoughts, leaping in the same out of
control way, possessed Sonya.

Just how far has the rift separated Dan and

my uncle? Could Dan, knowing Alex would be blamed, have set the warehouse on fire himself . . . for some demoniac vengeance?

No! Even if the affection that had once been solid between them had turned to hatred, Dan would not be capable of this.

Dan's low voice, sounding more sorrowful than censorious, broke into her solitude. "What if he is involved?"

"Uncle Alex has never done anything illegal," she said, her voice shaking. "I can think of others far more likely to be guilty."

"Alex is in bad need of cash, or he wouldn't even consider selling Mother's place."

"Regardless, Alex would never resort to fraud."

"I don't know whether he's responsible or not and neither do you. But I do know one thing; I'm not going to let him drag you into this."

Sonya, feeling dazed, turned away from him and started back toward the car.

Dan caught up with her and forced her to face him.

"Do you know what Alex told the sheriff? He said you were with him all evening, from nine o'clock on." Strong fingers tightened on her arm. "That's a lie, isn't it?"

Sonya, feeling threatened by his words and

his authoritative manner, tried unsuccessfully to free herself. The shouts of the firemen, the milling crowd, and the crackling fire veneered an air of unreality on the scene.

"From what Alex has been telling him, the sheriff will think you planned this together. I want you to go right now and make your own statement. Tell Henry the truth, no matter what it is or who it implicates."

"No! Dan, let go of me!" Sonya shook loose from his grasp and half-ran toward the station wagon. Several people turned to watch her. She didn't glance around at Dan, who called sharply, "Sonya! Come back here!"

Alex was waiting in the car. She slid in quickly beside him. Irascibly he backed the station wagon around and headed toward home. Broodingly silent, he leaned forward as he drove, his gaze not once straying from the highway.

Sonya caught her breath enough to say, "They're thinking this is arson."

"I know," he answered, "and they're trying to railroad me."

"Someone was seen inside the warehouse."

"That's what they say."

"What did happen?" Sonya asked.

"I don't know any more about it than you do."

"They're going to think we set the fire to collect the insurance. How will we be able —"

Alex cut in.

"We're going to set tight and let them try to prove it." Uncle Alex's slow, steady words failed to calm her. "From nine o'clock on, you and I were together."

"But that's not true!"

Alex turned to her abruptly, his large, frosty eyes steady on hers. "Hang together," he drawled, "or hang alone."

"I can't lie to the police."

Despite making the remark she voiced with certainty, Sonya knew Alex expected her to back up his statement. Didn't he realize she was, after all, Sam Brighton's daughter, and lying was something Sam Brighton's daughter could never do, no matter what the consequences? She became suddenly resentful.

Alex shouldn't put me in this position.

From the open window a breeze blew her hair to disarray and cooled her skin. She watched field after field sweep past them.

A yard light gleamed brightly in front of the shed, making Alex's additions look more crude and makeshift set against the looming mansion. They walked to the house together. Alex's face, void of the droll humor that characterized him, seemed a little more worldly, a little less like the man who'd always protected her.

They parted immediately, and Sonya went upstairs to her room.

After a very long time, feeling restless and feverish, Sonya returned downstairs. A light gleamed from beneath the door at the far end of the front room. No doubt Alex, wanting to be alone, had retreated to his study. She wouldn't bother him.

Even before Sonya had pressed the switch and light filled the room, she knew someone was in the kitchen. Connie stood squarely in front of her. Her expression was composed, as if standing alone in the dark at this hour was nothing out of the ordinary.

Immediately Connie turned to the coffee maker, and the silent area soon became filled with the gurgling sound of filtering water.

"I came out for a snack," Connie announced, wiping her hands on her robe. "Do you want to join me?"

"I wouldn't turn down a cup of coffee."

Connie wore a long silk robe with silver

flowers. She wore it casually, the tie looped around her thick waist. It had been Anna's.

Sonya, thinking Connie would be able to detect her sudden repulsion, avoided her gaze. The events of the evening had worked on Sonya's mood. The anger she felt must surely be caused by more than seeing Connie lounging in Anna's robe.

Only a robe.

Connie couldn't know the sentiment behind it, hadn't helped Uncle Alex purchase it or seen the glow on Anna's face as she had opened her gift.

"Now what do you suppose I did with my cigarettes?" Connie continued looking around near the sink as she spoke. At last, she gave up her search with a shrug and seated herself heavily at the kitchen table.

Sonya, unable to overcome the distaste she felt for Connie and the casual way she could possess what was not hers, forced herself to make an effort at communication. "I've never seen such a fire."

"Those things happen," Connie replied. "Alex never even told me about it. He just gets you instead. I wouldn't have known at all if Mel hadn't stopped by, hunting for Alex."

"Mel?"

"Melvin LaVett. He's our neighbor. Alex's

best friend."

"Oh, yes, I met him today."

"Poor Mel. Honestly, I feel sorry for him."

Sonya recalled nothing about the bronzed, happy neighbor to inspire any pity, but too upset by the fire to be concerned with anything else, didn't inquire why.

Connie told her anyway.

"Trying to make a living on that old farm. It's hard to believe. No one's even lived on it for years. He's a real good mechanic."

Sonya couldn't help but find Connie's chatter annoying, but the woman prattled on.

"Alex always talks about setting him up with a garage. Really, though, Mel's not as good at fixing cars as Emil is. Emil can just fix anything. I told Alex that. It looks as if he'd want to take care of us first."

Connie smirked as she spoke, offended over some casual plan of Alex's that was never likely to materialize. "But that's Alex for you."

Connie brought a hand up from the pocket of Anna's robe.

"They were here all the time."

She laid the package of cigarettes between them on the table. As she took out a lighter, her blue eyes raised to Sonya's.

"You and Alex sure do gab a lot."

"We always have."

"Not him and me. We get along like a cat and a dog. Alex always starts in about something, and pretty soon we're slugging it out. Say, I almost forgot, someone called here for you."

"Do you know who?"

"Jody Fry. Actually she wanted to talk to Alex, but I told her you were here, too. Then she wanted to talk to you. She said she'd call back."

The last person in the world Sonya wanted to see now was her cousin, Jody.

"Alex wasn't very happy about it when I told him. Guess he doesn't like her very much. Anyway, Jody said she'd be in town before long."

Sonya knew that Jody, unpredictable and irresponsible, was certain to cause even more problems for Alex and her. Feeling even more apprehensive, she rose and poured the coffee.

Even though it must be very late, Sonya could hear the frequent sweep of traffic from the highway. Connie's lapse of conversation provided her with an opportunity to again mention the fire.

"What do you think caused the warehouse to burn?"

"I certainly wouldn't know the answer to

that, Sonya. But, if I were you . . ."

Her words trailed off at the sound of the front door opening and closing and heavy footsteps moving across the room.

"Connie!" a harsh voice burst out.

"What is it?"

"Where's Alex?" Emil appeared at the kitchen door. The glaring light emphasized his massive shoulders, the thickness of his neck and lips. He spoke slowly, as if he'd planned in advance the exact words he would use.

"I thought he'd be at his desk, but he isn't there. I've looked everywhere for him. Where do you suppose he's gone?"

Sonya rose, her legs feeling almost to weak to hold her.

"Is his car here?"

"Yes."

Connie looked from Sonya to Emil.

"We'd better hurry and find him," she said. "With all this excitement, Alex just might have had another stroke."

CHAPTER 6

After racing through the empty rooms of the mansion looking for Uncle Alex, Sonya left the house in panic and headed toward the workshed. Through the wide-open door a single, harsh glow of overhead bulb lighted the disorderly arrangement of tools scattered across the work table, the chair with a broken rocker that set on top of furniture covered with old blankets. Her gaze rested for a moment on the wind-up phonograph that Alex used to play for Dan and her when they were children.

She'd half-expected to find Alex slumped on the cement floor, not because of a fatal stroke, but murdered. Even though the shed was vacant, fear roared around her like the flames that had consumed the warehouse.

Sonya felt certain that Alex had been out here tonight. He'd doubtless figured out who'd burned the warehouse. Because he knew the arsonist was aware of his knowledge, Alex, in order to protect himself, must have decided to disappear, to work behind the scenes until he could gather proof to take to the sheriff. If this had happened, chances were they were dealing with an extremely dangerous person.

He might even have killed Alex and disposed of his body.

The thought caused Sonya to shudder and turn away. She must find Dan. She started running, but stopped short before she reached her car.

Where did I leave my keys?

Not wanting to return to the house, feeling too distraught to drive, she set out on foot toward Dan's cabin.

The darkness confused her, the field a black void stretching endlessly ahead. Occasionally she stumbled on clods or rocks, but each time forced herself to continue at the same fast pace. Dan's strong hands seemed to reach out to her from across the field.

Even the gentle climb upward challenged her waning strength, but once the land leveled again, her steps became faster, more certain, and the cabin neared quickly.

As she drew closer, she noted the dark windows and the fact that Dan's car was not parked in front. Tears filled her eyes.

Although she knew it was of no use, she still pounded on the door and circled the place to make certain the car was gone.

Why isn't Dan here?

She refused to allow any answers to form in her mind.

As she headed back to the mansion, the blackness around her seemed complete and all-absorbing. The more distance she put between herself and the cabin, the worse it became, especially her sense of aloneness.

Where's Alex? Will I ever see him again, ever hear his crusty, teasing voice?

His great affection, imperfect but immense, had always been a mainstay in her life.

I mustn't assume he's dead.

He hadn't taken his car, but if he'd felt threatened, he naturally would have called on some friend to help him.

Sonya couldn't keep from seeing images of the burning warehouse, from seeing Alex's form enclosed in fire. She tried hard to control her runaway thoughts. To repress them she began counting her steps — eighteen, nineteen, twenty. The counting became a force propelling her forward — fifty, fifty-one.

Headlights broke abruptly through the darkness.

Dan!

Relieved, she turned and watched the vehicle until she made out its outline, large and heavy, seeming to creak with age. The lights jogged closer until they fell across her path.

The pickup groaned to a stop. A dark figure leaned across the seat to open the door. An amazed voice asked, "What are you doing out here?"

Melvin LaVett.

As she climbed in beside him, the dash light illuminated his lean, suntanned face. He looked different without the large, carefree smile, without the gleam of strong, white teeth. A frown now cut deeply across his brow.

"Connie called me," he said. "Has Alex been found?"

She shook her head.

Sonya noted the tensing of the hard muscles in his jaw. He remained silent as they approached the house, now a flood of lights.

A short, heavy man wearing a pale gray uniform stood in the yard near Alex's shed. The moment Melvin switched off the ignition, the uniformed man strode over to meet them. He wore a silver badge reading 'Sheriffs Department, Baxter County'.

"Sonya Brighton?" he asked, as he peered into the window. "I've been wanting to talk to you."

Melvin's arm supported her as they followed the sheriff into the house. Once in the well-lighted front room, his hair and face looked almost the same color — golden brown.

"This girl has been through quite a lot tonight," he said firmly. "She's in no shape to talk to anyone.

The cop wasn't to be side-tracked.

"If we're going to find Mr. Brighton, we need all the assistance we can get."

The stocky man opened the door to Alex's study and patiently waited for Sonya to enter. She glimpsed Melvin's face, grim and frowning, before the sheriff closed the door shutting him out.

Sonya hadn't been in Alex's study for many years. When Anna was alive, she had referred to it as the library and it was entered only by invitation. The windup phonograph, the love seat, the velvet drapes were gone; only an ample supply of pictures made the room seem less than bare.

"Perhaps you don't remember me? I'm Henry Davis."

His large hand tightened around hers.

'Handshaking Henry,' that's what Alex al-

79

ways called him.

"All he ever does is shake hands and grin," Alex would be sure to say whenever the sheriff's name was mentioned. Henry Davis was smiling at her now. An ineptness was apparent about him that at any other time she might not have noticed.

"Of course I remember you," she said.

"Connie Brighton was very upset when she called me. Do you have any idea where your uncle might be?"

"No."

"Since his car's here, perhaps a friend picked him up. Do you know of anyone in particular we should contact?"

"It's been a number of years since I've been in Linnville."

Sonya paused, then said, uncertainty gripping her voice, "He's been gone only a short while. I'm sure I'll be hearing from him soon."

Davis ran a finger along Alex's desk as though checking for dust.

"Under ordinary circumstances, I'd agree with you. But given what's taken place, I thought I'd see if I could find him tonight. According to the others, you were the last person to have seen him." The sheriff looked at his watch. "When was it? Three hours ago?"

"Yes." Sonya leaned forward, both hands gripping the arms of the chair.

"Do you believe he's been harmed?"

"It's something to consider."

He spoke the words as if he thought this possibility was very remote. "Mrs. Brighton thinks . . ."

His voice trailed off and he leaned back in the swivel chair behind Alex's desk, shirt stretching tight around his ample stomach.

"I want to talk to you mainly about the way the warehouse burned."

"We shouldn't be concerned with that now, not with Uncle Alex missing."

"The two are interlocked. That's why you must answer all of my questions."

"Are you even sure the fire was arson?"

"Without doubt. Gas cans were found in the rubble. It was a very sloppy job, one done by an amateur."

"Then that eliminates Uncle Alex. He never does sloppy work."

"But probably he's in no condition to do what was required," the sheriff countered, then added, "So . . . he might have hired someone to set it for him."

"He wouldn't do that. And neither would I."

On the surface, her statement seemed to satisfy him. Henry Davis' eyes were a very light gray — kind eyes, she thought. He eased his bulky form forward as he spoke.

"I want two things. For you to trust me, and for there to be truth between us."

Sonya hadn't expected this. It was almost as if he'd already anticipated her lying in order to protect Uncle Alex from being the major suspect in an arson case and was trying to prevent any false statements before they occurred. Yet he didn't look that perceptive.

Henry Davis lapsed into a lingering stillness. He was purposely allowing her time, time to think before she spoke. His actions surprised her and at the same time predisposed her to like and respect him.

When he did speak, he talked about her father.

"I always admired Sam Brighton very much," he said.

The fondness in his voice altered a little when he mentioned Alex.

"The first time I saw your uncle, I was out soliciting for votes. He invited me in for coffee. While we were socializing, he told me he wasn't going to vote for me." He smiled a little. "I didn't like hearing that, but, all the same, truthfulness never fails to impress me."

Sonya wished he'd get to the point. She

felt very tired and he seemed so obviously vying for her confidence. She rubbed a hand across her forehead. "Maybe it would be better if we would talk later," she suggested.

"When I asked for you earlier, Mrs. Brighton told me you'd left. Where did you go?"

"I went after Dan, to tell him we couldn't find Uncle Alex."

"Wasn't Mr. Rathmell at home?"

"No."

"Would Alex Brighton and his son be together?"

Remembering the fierce burning in Dan's eyes when he'd spoken of Uncle Alex at the warehouse, she said, "Dan isn't Alex's son. He was half raised when Alex married John Rathmell's widow, Anna Rathmell. No, I'm sure they wouldn't be together."

The sheriff leaned forward on his elbows.

"Your uncle and you were partners in Brighton Furs, I understand."

"My uncle and my father. The store and warehouse has been closed since Father's death a little over a year ago. Dad's estate is not yet settled."

"You're Sam Brighton's only heir, though, so we can say this business belongs to your uncle and you."

"That's correct."

"I understand your uncle and you were

together this entire evening before the fire."

Sonya didn't want to lie to him, yet if she told him that Alex and she were not together, he would assume that Alex was involved in the arson. It seemed of utmost importance that the sheriff believe her uncle to be innocent, for this would change the way the sheriff viewed Alex's disappearance.

"Were you with him?" Henry Davis prompted.

Sonya, to avoid lying, responded with a question.

"What time did Tom Bradley see someone inside the warehouse?"

"Five minutes after ten."

"Did he identify anyone?"

"As a matter of fact, he saw only the gleam of a flashlight."

The sheriff's large hands, folded together on the desk, clamped and unclamped.

"Did your uncle or you go to the warehouse this evening before it was discovered to be on fire?"

"No."

"Are you speaking for both of you?"

Sonya's silence hung guiltily over the room. She finally answered, "Yes."

The expression of benevolence abandoned the sheriff's face, and although he said nothing, she could feel the wordless clash between them. After a long length of time, apparently deciding upon another approach, he asked, "Did you come back to Linnville in order to settle your father's estate?"

"I came back to see Uncle Alex. We were going to take this opportunity to settle Dad's affairs."

"Furs. That's an odd business to start in the Midwest, in Kansas."

"Dad was certain trade would build up in time, but, I think you're right — the location worked against it."

"Was the business solvent?"

Smacked with the implications of his question, Sonya hesitated. Then, "No, it hadn't been for the last few years of operation. We intended to take a loss on the final settlement."

The sheriff's eyes appeared to have lost their width and grayness.

"But now, since the fire, that won't be necessary."

Sonya's gaze dropped from Henry Davis' large, accusing eyes to his hands, still folded in front of him on the desk. He wore a simple, gold band, tight enough to cause a bulging around his finger.

The sheriff's sudden stillness unnerved her. Could he actually believe Alex and she had plotted this fire?

"While looking for Mr. Brighton, his wife unlocked his station wagon. Did your uncle usually carry extra gas in his car?"

Sonya's heart began to race.

"He wouldn't start a fire with gasoline, if that's what you're asking. He'd know that it would be much too easily traced."

The sheriff leaned forward slightly.

"Just what method would he use to set a fire? Did you and he ever discuss that?"

Sonya's face flushed. She wasn't going to allow him to intimidate her.

"I don't think I'm going to talk to you anymore," she said, "not without a lawyer."

CHAPTER 7

The moment the sheriff left Alex's study, the quietness in the room seemed to spring alive with crackling flames. After the fire this evening Sonya shouldn't have left her uncle alone. If Uncle Alex had fought with someone tonight, if the fight had gotten out of hand . . .

She couldn't prevent intruding images from arising, of a killer dragging Alex's body from the shed — of a freshly dug grave.

Sonya rose and paced around the room. Feeling more ill than before, she sank at last into the swivel chair behind Uncle Alex's desk. The bottom drawer, crudely secured by a hasp and padlock, would doubtlessly contain, as it always had, Alex's Smith and Wesson revolver — unless that, too, was missing.

Alex's being gone, Sonya told herself sternly, didn't mean that he'd been harmed. A greater possibility existed that he'd known who had burned the warehouse and for his own protection had chosen to disappear. He wouldn't believe Sonya was in any danger, only him. And if that was the case, Uncle Alex would need to remain hidden. The fact that he hadn't taken his own vehicle suggested that someone had picked him up, some trusted friend, some old army buddy, like Bill Cole.

Rummaging through the desk drawers, Sonya located a leather address book. She found Bill's number scribbled on the inside cover. If Alex had turned to anyone for help, it would be Bill Cole, a retired trucker who at one time delivered for the company. With shaking hand she dialed the number and waited, visualizing Bill Cole's dark, thin face, deeply etched around unsmiling mouth and eyes. Even though his hair was gray, he wore it close-cropped, as he had when his old army photos had been snapped. Somehow, despite his age, she would always picture him in fatigues, an aging G.I. Joe.

Cole answered the phone.

"Hello," she said. "This is Sonya Brighton, Alex's niece. I'm sorry to call you so late, but I was wondering if you've seen Alex tonight."

She remembered well Bill Cole's cautious

attitude and heard it expressed now in his voice.

"I talked to him on the phone this evening, right after the fire."

"He called to tell you about the warehouse?"

A period of stillness followed. Then, "Alex was very disturbed."

"Do you have any idea where he might be?"

"He used to take to the road whenever anything went wrong. He's probably out driving around now." Bill Cole hesitated again. "No doubt he'll show up before long."

"But his car's here, Bill. I'm very worried about him. Can you think of anyone else I might contact?"

Alex's old friend became intensely silent. Finally, almost grudgingly, she thought, he replied.

"Let me do some checking. If I find out anything, I'll get back with you."

With little choice, Sonya agreed, then hung up and skimmed through the other names in the book, most of them totally unfamiliar to her. She couldn't make random calls this time of night; they would have to wait until morning.

She slipped into the front room. The lone

table lamp near the couch cast shadows over the trio gathered around the sheriff.

"This Wilbur lives at the Falcum Boarding House on Paramount and Eleventh," Henry Davis was saying — repeating, probably, what Emil had just told him.

"Emil always spends a lot of time with Freddy Wilbur," Connie answered after a brief exchange of glance with her brother-in-law. "Freddy wants to be a wrestler. He wants Emil to teach him — to manage him," she corrected.

"You were in Kansas City with Wilbur all evening, then, from six o'clock until you returned home just after twelve?"

"Yes," Emil agreed. "The shed lights were on, so I stopped to look in. I had some things to discuss with Alex, so when I didn't find him there, I began searching for him."

The sheriff appeared to accept everything Emil told him without question. In fact, he didn't even seem very interested in Emil's alibi. Instead, he began talking affably about his own wrestling days, back in high school, and about how he had once watched Emil wrestle at Linnville's city auditorium.

Emil listened intently, heavy head bent. He wore, no doubt to impress Henry Davis, a drab, double-breasted suit that failed to adjust to his towering frame.

"Emil's a good wrestler," Alma sing-songed.

Emil stared past Alma to Connie, saying bluntly, "I turned the job down."

"You should know best, Emil."

Sonya's spirits plummeted. The story Connie and Emil had cooked up about his being with Freddy Wilbur when the fire was set rang of falsehood. It looked as if it were contrived in order to clear Emil from all involvement concerning the warehouse fire, or to totally disassociate him with whatever had happened to Uncle Alex. The sheriff, without turning to look toward Sonya, nevertheless addressed her as she passed by him.

"We'll talk again in the morning."

Sonya, feeling increasing apprehension, slipped into the winding stairway. At the top of the steps in the long, dimly-lit corridor, she came face to face with Dan.

He hadn't changed clothes and the black smudge still darkened the side of his face. That, and his weariness, grim eyes, heavy-lidded, only added to his handsomeness.

"I've been looking everywhere for you." He didn't allow her time to speak. "Connie called and told me about Alex. Ever since then, I've been trying to find you. When you didn't answer my knock, I went into your room."

He released her arm and fumbled in the pocket of his shirt. He unfolded a sheet of paper ripped from the binder of a notebook. "I found this message lying on your bed."

Sonya scanned the large, scrawled letters.

"I'm okay. Don't tell anyone you've heard from me. I'll contact you later."

The quick, slanted lettering seemed weak and wobbly, as if the hand that had written it had shaken, or as if someone were trying to make it look that way. She had received so many letters from Alex.

Why can't I identify his handwriting with any degree of accuracy?

Of course, the recent stroke had affected Alex's right hand.

Sonya looked from the paper to Dan. His eyes, opaque and unreadable, watched her solemnly as he posed a question.

"Surely Alex isn't hiding out to keep from being charged with arson?" he asked.

"He wouldn't do that," Sonya replied. "If he left here, it was for another reason."

Dan gripped her arm again, the pressure tense like his features. "If Alex is in trouble, Sonya, you know, in spite of everything, that I'll help him."

His dark eyes seemed anything but reassuring. Was it Sonya's exhaustion, the promptings of her own fear, causing her to think that they were smoldering with some evil, fiery light?

But Dan's deep voice revealed his own worry — worry mingled with a hint of frustration.

"I'm going to drive around for a while and see if can find him. Do you have any idea where he might be?"

Sonya fought against tears threatening to surface.

"We don't even know for sure that he wrote this note."

"Who else would write it?"

"Someone who wants us to think Uncle Alex is alive and safe." Her voice caught in a sob. "What if something's already happened to him?"

"No. Nothing's happened to Alex. He can take care of himself. He always has."

"But this time it's not the same. He hasn't fully recovered from his illness. And those people downstairs . . . Dan, Alex is in real danger!"

"You just stay here. I'll get back with you."

No way.

"No, I'm going with you!"

Muffled voices, Emil's and the sheriff's, drifted from the kitchen as Dan and Sonya hurriedly left the house. They headed toward Linnville.

Sonya, sobered by their impossible task, watched quietly from the window. In the dead of night the rolling fields looked desolate and empty.

Slowly, watchfully, Dan drove up and down the main section of town where street lights glowed across vacant, limestone buildings. Only one car passed by them and they spotted no one on the streets.

"Not exactly Boston," Sonya commented.

"Which is good for us," Dan said. "Here everyone knows everyone else. If Alex has been in town tonight, someone's seen him. All we have to do is ask the right person."

They reached the edge of town, and Dan came up with a suggestion.

"Let's have a little talk with Carl."

He swung the vehicle in close to the all-night truck stop and went off in search of the man, but soon returned, looking even more weary than before. His words were edged with deep discouragement.

"I thought if anyone would have spotted Alex tonight, it would have been Carl."

He backed the car away from the building, slowly now, as if he were ready to give up. They crept along the twisting highway toward Alex's house. Dan pulled into the driveway, but didn't stop. They passed the

shed and jogged across the dark trail leading toward the barn.

"Where are you going?"

"Let's check out the old Bailey place."

"You mean the farm that Melvin LaVett's
rented?"

At the mention of LaVett's name, a muscle
tightened in Dan's jaw.

"LaVett drifted into town not long ago.
Alex immediately took a liking to him. For
some reason or other the two of them have
become as thick as —" Dan stopped his
sentence abruptly. He didn't add, 'as
thieves', but the words and their implication
hung in the air.

Sonya lost no time giving what had by
now become an automatic response.

"Alex had nothing to do with starting the
warehouse fire." She paused, noting the
doubtful look on Dan's face and added
convincingly, "Even if he had, he would
never involve anyone else. If Alex wanted
the warehouse burned, he'd have burned it
himself."

"Unless it were someone else's idea."

"You mean Melvin's? Alex couldn't afford
to pay him much. What would he gain by
it?"

"I just don't trust LaVett. A man like him
has no one's interests in mind but his own."

Dan didn't look at her as he drove. The car swerved as it followed the deeply rutted tracks.

Alex had told her that Melvin was with him when they'd found Anna's ring and the other jewels in Dan's cabin.

Could Dan be thinking that Melvin robbed Alex himself and planted the jewelry in his house? If it had been planted.

She glanced at Dan's profile, the strong lines reflecting so much character and strength. She immediately reversed her thoughts. Someone had tried to frame Dan for the robbery, someone with a definite purpose in mind, with much to gain if he could manage to separate Dan and Alex. Logically, who else could that be but Emil and Connie?

Melvin, seeing the situation, had merely come to Alex's aid.

"Melvin seems very helpful," Sonya said, "It's not fair to jump to conclusions."

"Then we won't. But Alex does perceive LaVett as his friend. So isn't it possible that Alex has talked LaVett into hiding him out?"

"But why?"

"That's what we'll find out when we locate Alex."

Beyond the barn they linked with a black-top road. Dan drove about a mile, then turned into a long, unkempt driveway overhung with thick cottonwoods.

The Bailey farm had once been important — Tim Bailey had been one of the county commissioners — but as Sonya glimpsed the aged, frame house through branches, she could see it had deteriorated almost beyond repair.

A yard-light illuminated the driveway, casting a spooky glow across the tree-enshrouded yard, across the dilapidated outbuildings. She saw a light inside the house, at a back window, but Melvin's truck was nowhere in sight.

"Look over there," Dan said, pointing toward a ruined shed where an old, black Ford set facing the house. "That's Emil Steelman's car. What could he be doing here?"

Dan got out.

"I'm going to take a look around."

His announcement caused an intense fear to grip Sonya. Fear for Dan, for herself. She didn't want to be left alone.

"Wait, I'll go with you."

But Dan had already strode off, disappearing around the corner where a sagging back porch extended from the main house.

Sonya started after him, but the sound of a motor caused her to stop, to whirl around.

Headlights from the black Ford Dan had recognized as Emil Steelman's fastened on her, momentarily blinding her.

As the car shot forward and careened toward the driveway, Sonya got the impression of a lone figure hunched over the wheel. Caught momentarily in the glow of yard-light, a frightened face peered out at her — the face of Alma Steelman!

CHAPTER 8

Alma sat rocking back and forth in the chair beside the front door waiting for Sonya to return. Her large eyes, filled with immense fright, locked on Sonya as she stopped beside her.

"What were you doing at the old Bailey place?" Sonya demanded.

"I was waiting for Melvin." The rocking stopped and Alma bent forward as if struck with a sudden illness. Her voice, almost a moan, became so low Sonya could barely make out her words. "I just wanted Melvin to find Alex right away."

"Why? Do you think my uncle is in danger?"

"Because Connie wants him found," Alma said, tears forming in her eyes. "I didn't do anything wrong. I just went over there. I just wanted to help."

"You startled me, that's all. I didn't even know you drove."

"Connie taught me how to drive." Alma brightened momentarily, but retreated quickly into the same heavy gloom. "Emil doesn't let me take his car. You won't tell him, will you? I didn't do anything I shouldn't do."

"No, I won't tell him," Sonya said gently. Once she'd reached the stairway, she turned back to Alma. "You can trust me, Alma. You can talk to me anytime, if there's ever anything you want to tell me."

Thoroughly puzzled by her encounter with Alma at the LaVett farm, Sonya returned to her room. Unable to rest, she once again studied the note Dan had given her. After many careful comparisons with a sample she had of Alex's handwriting, she still wasn't fully convinced he'd written the message.

But the chance existed that he had left her not knowing exactly what to do. Randomly she opened Alex's address book.

Should I just wait for Alex to contact me, or should I attempt to locate him by calling each person listed here?

She looked through the book, considering for a while a Kansas City address — 5674 W. Market Street — with no name or phone number beside it. In the end Sonya placed the note, supposedly from Alex, into the address book and hid it by balancing it behind the heavy wooden frame enclosing the portrait of John T. Rathmell.

Downstairs, not finding anyone in the house, she stepped out onto the porch. The cool, fresh air began to drive away her indecision. She'd never find Uncle Alex if he didn't want to be found. The best thing she could do was investigate the cause of his disappearance — the fire. Although it would probably be futile, the first chance she got, she'd drive to Kansas City and talk to Freddy Wilbur about Emil Steelman's alibi.

Melvin LaVett's old, blue truck was parked in the driveway, but Alex's neighbor was nowhere around. Sonya looked beyond the truck toward the rolling fields and the gray, twisting strip of highway that would eventually join the interstate. An ancient van with many scrapes and dents crept laboriously around the sharp curve. As it pulled into Alex's yard, smoke streamed from under the hood. The van chugged forward and came to a jerky stop just as it reached the workshed.

Sonya knew the driver would be her cousin Jody even before she caught sight of the pretty, freshly-scrubbed face and the pale, sunburned hair. Strands escaping from a careless knot dangled across her high cheeks and forehead. Although several years older than Sonya, Jody looked no different than she had looked in high school — still the exuberant teenager in faded jeans and ragged shirt. Sonya hadn't seen Jody since she had left her husband and had set off on a jaunt around lower California. Sonya's weariness increased at the sight of her cousin, who bounced from the van and bounded forward, shouting, "Hey, Sonya!"

"I heard you were in town." Sonya tried to sound friendly as she added, "It's been a long time."

"I'll say. Christmas before last. I was really surprised when Connie told me you were here."

Sonya cut in anxiously.

"Have you heard about the warehouse fire?"

"Who hasn't? The news is all over town! What a blaze! I drove by there this morning. It's still smoldering." Jody gave Sonya a quick hug. "I should have come right out yesterday when I first got to town." She glanced back disgustedly at the old van. "But I was having trouble with the beast."

Sonya drew in her breath. "We don't know where Uncle Alex is. He's been missing since last night."

"Missing? You're kidding, aren't you? Where would he go?"

Believing Jody would be as worried and upset as she was, Sonya started a long, involved answer, but Jody, gaze straying away from her, interrupted, exclaiming, "Who's that?"

Sonya, irritated by Jody's total lack of concern, turned to watch Melvin, looking rested and carefree despite last night's late hour, move agilely down the steps of the house toward them.

"Wow?" Jody said under her breath. "Is he yours?"

"He's Uncle Alex's neighbor." Sonya waited for Melvin to approach, then introduced him. "Melvin LaVett. Jody Meyers."

"Porter," Jody corrected. "I took my maiden name back." Her eyes lit as she appraised Melvin. "So he's not yours! Someone's, probably, though. That's always my luck."

Melvin, pleased over Jody's flattering comment, gripped her hand.

"Another niece?" His teeth gleamed very white against his tanned face. "Any more of you?"

Jody's hand lingered in his.

"No. When the Brighton family got to perfect, they quit." She appraised him, still

103

beaming. "Sonya's never mentioned you in her letters. Now I know why. She's keeping you for herself."

Melvin shot Sonya a playful look.

"I wish that were the case, but we just met yesterday."

Sonya glanced from Jody back to Melvin, wondering why Jody didn't at least pretend some interest in Alex's welfare.

"Is there any news about Alex?"

"No," Melvin replied, "the sheriff says he hasn't a single lead to follow."

"Let's run him off, then," Jody exclaimed, as if this were all some huge joke. "We don't need any sheriffs hanging around here. We can do his job ourselves."

Sonya turned away from her so Jody wouldn't see the displeasure she felt. Why did Jody have to choose this particular time to arrive? She always brought storm and havoc, but in the midst of all these problems, her being here was going to be unbearable.

Usually Sonya could overlook Jody's thoughtlessness, but today she couldn't. Sonya even found herself resenting the easy banter that had sprung up between her and Melvin LaVett . . . not that Jody noticed.

"My van won't run another foot," Jody was telling Melvin. "Do you know anything about motors?"

Melvin glanced dubiously at the vehicle. "I can take a look."

"Would you? Sonya and I'll take my bags to the house, then I'll be right back out and we'll get this monster running."

As Jody spoke, she opened the back door of the van and tossed out a couple of battered, canvas bags.

"Sonya, is that you?" Connie called from the kitchen as they entered the house. "Henry wants to talk to you. He's been waiting a long time in Alex's study."

Not again, Sonya thought tiredly, as she set Jody's bag beside the buffet.

Jody, windblown and disheveled, breezed past her. Emil and Alma sat at the table and Connie stood in front of the stove.

Jody tossed her shoulder-strap purse on a vacant chair and exclaimed, "So, where's my favorite uncle?"

Emil and Connie exchanged glances.

"I told you," Sonya replied, "no one knows where he is."

"Alex is just being Alex," Connie stated, her voice deeply critical. "He just doesn't care how much he worries everyone."

"He's bound to show up sooner or later," Jody replied indifferently.

Connie turned slowly from the stove,

spatula in her hand. "So you're Jody, Alex's other niece, the one I just talked to on the phone."

"That's me." Jody's inattentive gaze wandered around the room. "The old place looks like it could do with some paint. I just might be able to stay for a while and help out."

Her words were met with stony silence.

Jody, undaunted, continued to look around.

"The T.V. and the radio are just filled with news of the warehouse fire. The Brightons are finally famous. The whole town, maybe even the whole state, will soon know exactly who we are."

Sonya couldn't resist cutting in, saying a little sardonically, "We might even make the post office posters."

"Sonya's just like Alex, isn't she?" Alma blurted out. "Alex would have said that very same thing, wouldn't he, Connie?"

Emil shot a censorious glance toward his wife, then his cold stare riveted to Sonya. "You'd better not keep the sheriff waiting."

"I'll go with you," Jody offered with enthusiasm.

"No. He'll want to talk to me alone."

As Sonya entered the study, Henry Davis

rose with out-stretched hand. The grasp possessed a warmth she didn't read in to his fleshy face.

Reluctantly she seated herself in exactly the same place where she'd faced him just last night. Daylight made the room look more drab and worn, brought attention to the marred surface of the oak desk separating them.

Sonya studied the sheriff in silence, realizing that he, too, seemed different. She now recognized determination and purpose beneath the agreeable manner she had at first mistaken for ineptitude. For a case of what he would consider common fraud, he was doing much more than his office required. Either he was a very good sheriff, or he had some special reason for this rigorous, on-the-job attitude.

"I'm going about this in an unusual manner," he told her, as he leaned forward slightly in Alex's swivel chair. "Even though the length of his absence doesn't merit it, I have my full force out looking for your uncle."

He paused, and to explain his action, added, "I don't like the fact that he hasn't contacted anyone. It seems very strange that, in spite of the fact that I've tried very hard, I've failed to locate him."

Sonya thought of the note hidden upstairs in her room. Genuine or not, it made her feel guilty, as if she were concealing from him something he had a right to know.

"I need the names of all the people who have keys to the warehouse."

Sonya hesitated.

"Only Alex and I . . . possibly Bill Cole, who still does odd jobs for Alex. There are others, though, who would have had access to Alex's keys."

"Where did Mr. Brighton keep his warehouse keys?"

"Probably on his key ring."

"You mean the one where he keeps his car keys? Mrs. Brighton gave me those and identified each of them for me. The warehouse keys weren't among them."

"Then I don't know where they are."

"There's another strange thing," Henry Davis said. "We found no fingerprints at all on the gas cans in Mr. Brighton's car. Whoever handled those containers must have worn gloves."

Sonya's eyes locked on his, meeting the challenge implicit in his slow-spoken words.

"My uncle had nothing to do with burning the warehouse. And neither did I."

The sheriff settled back into the chair.

"Much of the insurance money will be

needed to cover business debts, isn't that what you said?"

"Yes."

"Brighton's Furs is a survivorship operation," he went on. "That means if some . . ." He paused, choosing his words carefully, "misfortune were to befall your uncle, you'd receive his share of the insurance money."

"What are you implying by that?"

Henry Davis' gaze left hers and wandered around the room. Instead of answering her question, he remarked, "I understand your uncle is planning to sell this house and land. I understand Connie Brighton is dead-set against it."

"Uncle Alex wouldn't need her consent to sell it. Anna's death left only his name on the deed."

Henry Davis leaned forward, asking, "Did you and your uncle quarrel over his wanting to sell out?"

"His decision to sell his own property has nothing to do with me."

"Oh, I think it has a lot to do with you. Many people would kill to own a place like this, free and clear."

His use of the word 'kill' started a pounding in Sonya's heart. When she'd at first been unable to find Alex, she'd believed he'd been murdered! What if that had actually happened? Fear and grief gave way to a moment of panic. She tried to force a calmness into her voice as she said, "His wife will inherit from him, not me."

Gray eyes, colder now, returned to her. "Not when your name is on the deed." The volume of his voice became louder, almost harsh. "You know as well as I do that Alex Brighton deeded this estate to you one month before his marriage to Connie Sims."

The shock of the sheriff's news slowly settled over her.

"I had no idea Uncle Alex deeded this place to me."

"Evidently Mrs. Brighton didn't know about it either. I found out this morning by checking at the courthouse. Did you agree to signing the deed recently so he would be able to sell?"

Alex had never discussed the sale of the Rathmell place with her. That meant only one thing: he had never actually been intending to sell it. The whole 'For Sale' business was a ruse, part of a plan to free himself from Connie and from Emil and Alma.

"You didn't answer my question."

"I would honor his right to the property even if my name was on the deed. He would know that."

"So you deny having any disagreement about his selling the property legally deeded to you?"

"We never discussed it."

"What you're saying, Miss Brighton, is that your uncle, without ever consulting you, put this place up for sale? This mansion he'd not even bothered to let you know was yours?"

Sonya faltered before his skeptical gaze. Alex had left her everything of real value that he owned.

Why didn't he tell me about it?

She wondered who else knew she was legal owner of the Rathmell place. *Does Dan know?*

The full impact of what Alex had done increased her awful sense of dread and burden. Ownership of the Rathmell place, however much unwanted by her, was going to arouse untold hatred and resentment in others, in the trio trying to take over her uncle's property — and certainly in her cousin Jody.

And what about Dan? How will he react to this information?

"What led Mr. Brighton to believe you would agree to the sale?"

Weakness stole over her.

"He trusts me, or he would never have

deeded it to me in the first place. No matter whose name is on the deed, I would consider it his."

"And he married Mrs. Brighton with her believing he still owned this property?"

Alex, suspecting that Connie was marrying him only to acquire this house and land, had done exactly what Alex would do — he'd secured it first.

"Alex has always been very independent," she said. "He seldom, if ever, seeks advice or lets anyone else know what he's doing."

"There's lots of talk around Linnville," Henry Davis said, his voice now chatty and conversational. "Rumor has it Mr. Brighton is very short on cash. A few bad years of farming, a lot of illness. No real use borrowing money to keep operating a venture that can no longer maintain itself. It looks as if he was being forced to sell out. Either that or find some immediate way to increase his assets."

So they were back to the arson again. Sonya felt panic close around her, but not because of Henry Davis' accusations. Sonya could read in the solemn way the sheriff was looking at her that he didn't expect Uncle Alex to be found alive.

And he could be right. The message hidden upstairs may not have been written by

Uncle Alex, but by his killer. But why would Uncle Alex write a note, when he could easily have talked to her before he left? The only possible answer would be that he had been unable to locate her and had felt it necessary to leave here in a hurry.

If Alex had gone into hiding, he would do so to avoid the danger involved in attempting to stay here and at the same time prove one of these people guilty of the arson and robbery. She consoled herself with the thought that when Alex did show up again — if he showed up again — he'd likely have in his possession some information that would clear them.

The sheriff's continued stillness, the steady focus of his gaze, unnerved her. Sonya could tell by the guarded look in his eyes exactly what he was thinking: *Thieves do fall out. That's why she murdered him.*

CHAPTER 9

"Sonya?"

She immediately recognized Dan's deep voice, resonant over the phone. He continued.

"I want you to meet me at the pond at twelve. Can you do that?"

She hesitated.

"I must see you, Sonya. It's very important. Please be there."

A click sounded on the other end of the line, giving her no chance to reply.

Why didn't he suggest meeting at Malroy's, or one of the other places in Linnville they'd so often frequented? Why did he select the total isolation of the pond?

Even as these questions plagued her, Sonya showered and then selected beige slacks and a yellow, silk blouse. As a final touch, she put on an amber necklace, whose dark depths highlighted the lighter hues of her blouse. She stepped away from the mirror, rearranging her hair, gleaming a glossy charcoal black.

Sonya slipped through the quiet house and outside. Melvin must have fixed the battered van for it no longer sat in the yard. Her problems would compound now that Jody was staying here. Great trouble would erupt the minute Jody found out that Alex had chosen to deed the entire Rathmell place solely to her.

Alex had thought enough of Anna to protect her property from the greed that had arisen to encircle it the moment he had fallen ill. This rural mansion had been Anna's life, or more nearly correct, the memory of John T. Rathmell had been, and Alex, with his earthly grasp of things, was very much aware of it. On the surface Alex appeared hard and cynical, but Sonya had seen the way Alex had always honored Anna, accepting responsibility, and always carrying out his duty to her. For many years he'd probably been doing whatever he had to do, dabbling in unorthodox methods of cash and credit, to keep the estate intact. But Sonya was not convinced, even after Alex had suffered the stroke, that he'd actually intended to sell out. Her name on the deed and the fact that he'd not even talked to her about the sale supported this belief.

All the evidence pointed to her uncle's being behind the arson, intending to use the quick cash from the insurance money as a means of hanging on. Yet, in her heart, Sonya believed in his innocence.

But was Alex safe now? Should she confide in Dan what the sheriff had told her? Feeling half-sick from anxiety, Sonya decided it would be best to remain silent.

Half way across the wide field, she realized she was inappropriately dressed. Strong, Kansas sunshine beat down relentlessly upon her. Occasionally a slight breeze stirred, stiflingly warm and dry, as if it blew from a furnace. Stillness filled with layers of heat was now-and-then mercifully broken by the strong, sweet notes of a meadow lark.

She reached the ridge and started down through tangles of underbrush. A group of birds flew in fright from her, the sound, sudden and alarming. She stood at the pool's edge looking through the thick foliage for a glimpse of Dan.

Sonya waited for what seemed like a long while, but Dan didn't appear. At first, uneasy and a little frightened, she began to think she was being watched. Her gaze kept wandering back up the slope of the ridge, but the only movement she could detect was the slight stirring of branches.

The slow passing of time in this warm, familiar place began at last to relax her. She knelt beside the water, raised a handful of liquid and watched it trickle through her fingers. Muddy, but because of the shade, cool. A deep blue dragonfly settled on a battered sumac stock that grew close to the water, clinging gracefully before gliding across the pool. Sonya followed its flight and saw beyond the dragonfly, across the pond, Dan leaning against the branch where he used to dive. She wondered how long he'd been watching her.

Their gazes met across the water. Dan smiled, waved, then gestured to her. Sonya slowly encircled the large pond, avoiding, because of her fragile sandals, the rocks embedded in the uneven ground. Dan's eyes lit joyfully as he stepped forward and caught her hands.

"Last night you looked so doubtful about that note. When I left you, I did my very best to check it out."

"You mean you've found Uncle Alex?"

"No, but I know now that he's alive and safe." Dan chuckled. "I must've talked to everyone in Linnville. Finally I got lucky. Early this morning, I found someone who'd seen him."

Dan's hands tightened around hers. In the

depth of his dark eyes she recognized the same sense of relief she herself felt.

"Alex left on his own, Sonya, so you don't have to worry about him. He's perfectly all right."

"Who saw him?"

"George Malroy, at the cafe where we used to hang out. George said he was getting out of his car when he noticed Alex driving by."

"Who was with him?"

"Do you remember Bill Cole? He used to deliver for Alex and your father. They were driving Bill's old truck last night, past Malroy's, heading toward Talbert."

"Did you tell this to the sheriff?"

Dan paused.

"If Alex thought it was best to disappear, let's just leave it that way. George agreed with me on that."

Sonya met Dan's steady gaze. His words were proof, weren't they, that he didn't really hate Uncle Alex? She found herself smiling back at him, grateful for all the trouble he'd taken, wanting to believe that in him she had a dependable ally.

"I thought I'd drive into Kansas City early tomorrow morning," she confided. "Emil's established an alibi there for the time the fire was set. I don't believe he was in Kansas

City. I'm going to find this Freddy Wilbur and talk to him myself."

"Probably it won't do any good. But I want to go with you."

"Let's meet, then, about seven o'clock tomorrow," Sonya suggested, stepping away from him.

"You surely don't intend to leave me right now? And ruin everything? I've gone to a lot of work especially for you."

What does he mean?

As if in answer, Dan took her arm and led her to a clearing where a card table was spread with a bright red cloth. Folding chairs were placed on either side, and nearby set a huge, wicker basket. At once Dan busied himself with plates, silverware, and containers of food.

A picnic? With Alex gone and with both he and me being framed for arson?

Bright, glaring sun couldn't directly penetrate the shade, but waves of heat did, making the air around them heavy and steamy. Dan seemed not to notice. "Don't look so shocked," he said. "You have to eat, anyway. Why not here?"

He pulled out the chair and waited for her to be seated. Despite the casual surroundings, Sonya felt suddenly very formal. She brushed at dust the field crossing had caused to settle on her light-colored slacks, aware of her own breathing and of the faint stirring of water caused by some inhabitant of the pond.

"If I remember correctly, you love fried chicken," Dan said. Baked beans, potato salad — she was suddenly very hungry for the first time since she'd arrived in Linnville.

Dan passed food to her, unmindful of filling his own plate. He had a way of looking at her, as if she were of such great importance to him. She sampled the food.

"Everything is perfect. You really can cook."

He laughed.

"A wise man isn't flattered," he remarked. "Or is it a flattered man isn't wise?"

"Or do you need to distinguish between flattery and genuine praise?"

His black eyes sparkled.

"I believe you're as smart as you're pretty!"

"Flattery," Sonya said.

Dan helped himself to the chicken, but instead of eating, remained watching her.

"I'd forgotten how lovely the pond is," she said.

"I still hang around out here a lot. When everything gets too ugly for me."

Sonya's gaze followed the direction he looked, toward the deep center of the pool. As she did, she felt close to him: this place wasn't just his, it was hers, too. Their refuge.

She'd been so looking forward to seeing Dan again. Why did their reunion have to be ruined by the trouble that separated him and her uncle?

"I don't want you to think that I don't care anything about him," Dan said suddenly, as if they'd been sharing the same thoughts. "I'll admit that over the years I've done a lot of things wrong trying to adjust to Mother's remarrying. But I do respect Alex — he's always been more than fair to me. And, you know, I . . ."

He paused, then started again, ". . . I still want to help him, even if he did burn the warehouse."

"Do you really believe he set the fire?"

"Don't you?"

"I know Alex wouldn't be fool enough to leave gas cans all over the place." Sonya lifted the cup of coffee to her lips. Right now she didn't want to think about Alex or arson or about her own predicament.

Almost as if he read her thoughts, his tone changed. "After we've eaten, I have a surprise for you."

"A surprise? Good."

Dan's conversation became light and airy. She found herself responding, feeling momentarily free.

After Sonya had finished the delicious apple cobbler, Dan pushed back his chair and rose quickly, saying, "Your surprise awaits."

Dan, reaching back to catch her hand, walked ahead of her. He led her around the tree, whose thick branch arched over the water, and wading into stocks of cattails that grew into the shallow water, announced, "Sonya, my boat!"

Sonya's stare fell to the rickety structure he called a boat. Giving a doubtful frown, she asked, "Are you sure it's seaworthy?"

"Of course." He added proudly, "I made it myself."

Sonya tried to convince herself that it would at least float, but it did seem put together somewhat shoddily — a flimsy, unpainted shell that definitely looked unsafe.

"What do you think?"

She couldn't crush his enthusiasm with the truth.

"Not bad."

"Wait till you see how easily it glides! It was simple to make," Dan said a little smugly. "It only took a couple of after-noons."

Sonya assessed it again, thinking it could have used many more hours of work.

"I've only had it out once. Sorry you missed the maiden voyage."

The eagerness in Dan's voice prohibited any negative replies.

"Let's try it out."

With a boyish zeal Dan pushed the wobbly boat around so she could step into it. As the boat creaked away from the bank, Dan gripped a handmade oar and guided it toward the deep center of the pond.

They passed shakily from shade into glaring sunlight. Brightness made the water look deeper, green and mucky. Water bugs skidded across the top.

"Maybe I should get into shipbuilding business."

Instead of responding to Dan's remark, Sonya tilted her head to listen.

Is that a gurgling sound?

She looked down at the floor of the boat. Water seeped through along the sides.

"Dan, maybe we'd better go back!"

At first he looked surprised, then puzzled, the way men do when they begin to notice their handiwork failing. The depth of the water began rapidly increasing. "It's leaking all along the side," Dan called. "There's no way I can stop it."

"Let's go back!"

Wielding the oar, Dan attempted to turn the waterlogged structure. Sonya didn't know whether it was the boat or herself that she heard moaning. His efforts only caused more water to pour in. Dan grinned.

"Hope you can swim!"

Sonya's ankles were already covered and the water level was rising fast. She cupped her hands and began quick, scooping motions.

"Bail, mate, bail!" Dan yelled merrily, deserting his oar and helping her. All the while, he laughed.

He thinks this is funny. He won't, when it sinks!

Despite all of their efforts the boat was becoming heavier, more lopsided. Warm, muddy water had soaked her slacks, although she'd still managed to protect her smart, silk blouse. Finally she stopped trying to bail water and shot Dan a lingering look of displeasure.

"We're sinking, sir!" she said sarcastically.

Dan chuckled. "Nothing to worry about! Your captain will save you!"

Sonya sat back and glared at him. At exactly that moment the boat submerged.

With startling speed, the footing dropped out from under her. She got a quick image of the sky and of Dan diving clear before tepid water swept over her. She went far under, clothes drawing tight around her.

When she came to the top, she was gasping and choking. Land looked a long way off. She drew in her breath and allowed the deep, warmish water to support her.

Dan splashed behind her.

"Thought you were a goner!" he yelled.

"Little you cared!"

Overhead the sun beat down upon the water, glaring against her eyes. Memories arose of Dan and she as children intent on racing each other to shore. The thought caused her to relax. With quick strokes Sonya headed toward the closest bank. Dan caught up with her easily, almost leisurely. He was enjoying this swim. The thought occurred to her suddenly that she was enjoying it, too. For a while she'd forgotten all else except Dan and their silly plight.

Dan swam so confidently, making her conscious of her hurried motions to stay above the water. He reached the bank first, extending his hand to her.

She refused his aid.

"Your assistance comes too late."

Her favorite blouse had been discolored

by the murky water, and her hair, styled so carefully, hung wet and stringy across her face. Dan's amused gaze wandered over her, and she felt a surge of irritation.

"Nothing like an invigorating swim!" Dan teased, rubbing his hands together. She started to move away from him, but he caught her and swung her back toward him. She felt his muscular body, dripping with pond water, pressed close to hers. Before she could struggle free, his lips had captured hers in a long kiss.

He laughed again; this time his laughter was startled, appreciative.

"Sonya," he said, "I believe you're in love with me!"

Ignoring his remark, Sonya spoke coolly, "Thanks for the picnic."

Then over her shoulder, feeling half-drowned and anxious to get back to the house, she added, "but not for the boat ride."

"You're not leaving already, are you?"

Sonya stopped midway up the path and looked back at him.

"I don't want to detain you. You've got some boat repair work to do."

Dan, sunlight falling across damp hair and clothes, looked very handsome.

"You're not afraid of me, are you?" he

asked, resuming his joking. "Afraid I'll try to kiss you again?"

She didn't reply to his questions, but before walking on, reminded him.

"Don't forget to meet me in the morning. At seven."

He didn't answer, made no offer to walk with her across the field.

Which added fuel to embers of annoyance. Sonya had known the boat wasn't going to float.

Why did I ever get into it?

Her mouth still felt the pressure of Dan's lips, and the excitement of the memory angered her for an instant.

What makes Dan take it for granted that I'm actually in love with him?

She slipped through the back entrance of the old house, hoping to find no one in the kitchen. The sheriff's voice stopped her.

"Miss Brighton," he said, amazed. "I didn't know it was raining."

She glared at him balefully.

"It isn't," she answered shortly. "I've been swimming."

CHAPTER 10

Jody must have been waiting in Sonya's room for some time. She sat cross-legged on the floor in front of the fireplace. The heat from outside had penetrated the room, and her skin looked pale and sweaty.

Without making a single inquiry about Uncle Alex and without even seeming to notice the condition of Sonya's wet hair and clothing, Jody asked, "Would you loan me some money, Sonya?"

"How much do you need?"

"I need a lot, but I could get by with a thousand dollars."

"That's quite a sum," Sonya remarked dryly.

Jody's eyes flashed angrily before she answered.

"I'm broke, that's all. I wouldn't come begging to you if it wasn't necessary! I must have cash right now, right away!"

Sonya studied Jody without speaking. She

had always dutifully sent Jody checks whenever Jody had requested money. Sonya had always written the debt off cheerfully enough, never expecting any return payment. She had done so because Jody had always meant a lot to her. But as she looked down at her now she wondered for the first time what she had meant to Jody. Had Sonya been only an ear for Jody's wild, sometimes untruthful stories, a sane counselor, a supplier of funds that bought . . . what? Usually Sonya had avoided asking, but this time she didn't.

"Why do you need so much money?"

Jody's wide, pallid forehead creased.

"I'm in some trouble, Sonya." Her voice raised in irritable protest.

"I don't see why I have to tell you all the details. Can't you just be a friend and make me a loan?"

Sonya studied her without speaking.

"The brakes are going bad in the van and it needs a new muffler. Everything's just gone wrong lately. You know I'll pay you back."

Jody's need for cash, Sonya decided, had nothing to do with repairing her vehicle.

For the first time Sonya noticed how very much Jody's eyes resembled Uncle Alex's, large and pale — although his eyes, unlike hers, were never frightened.

Jody sighed her exasperation.

"So you've got to hear it all. Okay, I'm in trouble," she muttered. "I'm in real trouble."

Sonya straightened up tensely. As she did, she glimpsed her own image in the ancient mirror above the dresser — wet, bedraggled, worried.

Selfish, maybe — but Sonya didn't want to hear about Jody's troubles now, not when she'd planned to go see Bill Cole right away and try to make contact with Uncle Alex.

Jody drew long legs up and hugged them, resting her head on her knees. Her pale blonde hair fell in streaks across the faded denim of her skirt.

"Those letters, the beach parties, the trips and fun I wrote about to you. They never happened. Since Mark and I broke up, I've just been trying to live, working in fast-food joints, never able to make enough to pay the bills. Everything's been just falling apart. I came to ask Alex for help, but I can see now that's not going to do any good."

Sonya, regarding Jody in the same intense way, remained alert to every change in Jody's large pupils, every slight expression from which she might be able to distinguish between Jody's truths and lies.

"What about Mark? He's always been willing to help you."

"I told you I left Mark. But, the fact is, Mark left me."

"Why, Jody?"

"He thought I was seeing someone else."

"Were you?"

"What difference does that make?" Jody's voice had lost its volume, and for the first time in their long association, she sounded defeated. "With Uncle Alex gone, all I have left is you. And, you . . . you're not going to help me, are you?"

"If you expect my help, you must be honest with me."

Jody averted her gaze.

"I've written some checks."

"Where?"

"Here. In Linnville. I have to pick them up, make them good, or they'll be turned over to the county attorney."

"Who did you write them to?"

"I gave one to Malroy's."

Sonya thought of George Malroy at the cafe. What an easy mark he would be for Jody's sob-stories.

"What's the exact amount you owe?"

"The last one I wrote to George was for two hundred dollars. But I need more, Sonya. I need a lot more!"

"I'll stop by and pick up the check you wrote to Mr. Malroy. That's the best I can do for you."

Jody jumped to her feet so quickly that Sonya stepped back.

"I knew you were going to let me down," she snapped with great animosity.

Sonya regarded her without speaking.

A strange calmness, more terrifying than the outburst, now possessed Jody.

"Before I came over here, I was asleep in my van. I had the worst dream. It was all about you! A real chiller."

An icy cast had moved into Jody's eyes. She backed towards the door as she spoke.

"I dreamed you were burning, just like the warehouse! A living torch! You were screaming for me to help you, but I couldn't! It was just . . . awful! I'm still trembling."

Her dream, Sonya decided, was just another lie Jody was making up, a way to lash out at Sonya by trying to frighten her. Despite this knowledge, Sonya felt a cold shiver run through her.

"Don't bother to stop by Malroy's," Jody said. "I'm sorry I even talked to you. I should never've asked you to do anything for me." Once Jody reached the door, she stopped.

"I don't like this woman Alex married. They, none of them, belong here. I think we should try to get them out."

She flounced off.

Sonya saw Melvin LaVett and Alma through the doorway of Alex's workshed. They were talking together in low voices, which ceased as she approached.

Sonya's sudden appearing upset Alma, who immediately, without a word, ducked by Sonya and plodded off toward the house. Melvin, lifting a screwdriver from the pile of tools on the work bench, crossed to the door.

"Alma wanted me to fix the hasp on the shed," he said. "She believes someone jimmied it loose."

"Did you tell the sheriff?"

"I don't think it's anything we need to tell him. The door's old and a little rotten. No doubt it pulled loose accidentally."

Sonya watched his strong, lean hands as they worked to refasten the metal strip to the door. He spoke to her over his shoulder.

"I keep thinking Alex will contact me — or you."

"I'm used to Alex's going off on his own."

Melvin stopped and turned to face her. "I've been worried about him. Alex just doesn't seem the type to run away."

"How long have you known him?"

He returned to his task, fingers deftly working as he talked.

"Alex befriended me when I first came to Linnville. That was a little over a year ago."

"Are you a native Kansan?"

Finished, he tossed the screwdriver back among the tools and wiped his hands on his jeans.

"I'm something of a drifter, but I claim California," he answered. "San Diego."

"That's where Jody lived last year."

Melvin smiled at the mention of her name.

"I'm surprised she made it back here driving that van. I managed to fix the carburetor, but that's only one of the problems."

"Jody's always been the daring one," Sonya replied, some of the old admiration she'd always felt for Jody sounding in her voice. "If she didn't have a vehicle, she'd still get to where she's headed."

Melvin smiled again, this time with the wide, happy smile that showed his strong, white teeth.

"She sounds just like me."

He lingered in the doorway. The last rays of daylight fell across his lean face, making him look like a hitchhiker from some sun-filled valley, and causing her to recognize how much Alex must have confided in him, how much Melvin LaVett and Uncle Alex were alike. Uncle Alex's love for Anna had bound him to the ordinary life, left him envying men like Melvin — foot-loose men, not entangled in failing businesses, deteriorating property, endless bills.

As if in response to her thoughts, Melvin said, "It was Alex who suggested I rent the Bailey place. I'd have moved on a long time ago if it hadn't been for him."

"You've helped my uncle a lot."

"He's someone I'll probably be one day," Melvin replied, grinning, "with a mind and body that doesn't fit together, a loner who detests accepting any help."

"Thanks for being there for him," Sonya said, relaxing some. "I wish I could've been here. I'd no idea how hard he's struggled to keep this place."

"Come right down to it, I never really thought he'd actually give it up."

As Melvin spoke, his gaze wandered to the 'FOR SALE' sign that set near the road.

"Alex does intend to move to that tiny house on Circle Street, though, mostly to free himself of Emil Steelman."

"Do you think Emil's the reason he left here?" Sonya asked.

"No, Alex isn't afraid of Emil." Melvin

spoke with certainty. "But he is afraid of someone."

The waning light playing across his face reflected in his eyes, now grown resolute.

"But don't worry, that someone'll have to get past me."

Sonya thought of Dan and a cold chill settled over her.

"People like Alex are always greatly loved and greatly hated," Melvin was saying. "Whoever this person is hates him enough to want to destroy him, and Alex knows it."

The knowledge he was referring to Dan caused Sonya to edge back toward her car.

"I'd better be going," she said.

"Sonya."

Melvin's voice held an edge of sharpness she'd never before associated with him.

"If Alex contacts anyone," he said, "it will be you or me. If you hear from him, you must let me know immediately. It might be very important to both Alex and you. Promise me you'll do that."

Only in Kansas could the weather alter with such rapidity. Dark clouds had gathered in the night sky, obscuring the full moon, and moisture hung heavily in the air.

The flat area of Linnville changed again to hills just east of the Smoky Hill. Mist followed the edge of the river, close to the ground. Once she'd crossed the bridge, Sonya turned off the highway onto an old dirt road. Just below a steep incline set the old Cole homestead.

Light from a pole in the yard disseminated into mist, leaving an eerie glow across the small, limestone house. Far back into the darkness she could make out the outline of a barn.

She parked among the jumble of wrecked cars and walked through the tall growth of weeds, wet from the mist. An unkempt air hung over the place, as if Bill Cole had done absolutely nothing to it since the death of his parents some twenty years ago.

Sonya found the door to the house unlocked.

If Dan had told her the truth, if Bill Cole were assisting Uncle Alex, then Alex might be using this isolated farm as a hiding place. If not, she might find evidence of Alex's having been here and that, alone, would set her mind at ease.

The door creaked as it opened. She switched on the flashlight she'd taken from her car and allowed it to play around the blackness, focusing on a table piled with car parts, then a sagging couch stacked with Capper's Weeklys and Linnville Journals.

She called out, "Alex!" once, then again. Her voice seemed to echo back from thick, stone walls.

Sonya avoided turning on the lights as she made her furtive search through the tiny rooms. She saw no sign that Alex had been here — only emptiness, total and complete. Prompted by a rush of fear, she retraced her steps, glad to be outside again.

As Sonya left the house, she was assailed with new suspicions. Wasn't it likely that Bill Cole and Uncle Alex were working together, that they had plotted to burn the warehouse? If they had, then Bill Cole would have to see some profit for himself in the deal. For the first time, the thought occurred to her that Bill might have removed the valuable stock, probably storing the expensive furs until they could be fenced at a grand profit.

But surely Uncle Alex would be no part of that scheme.

Nor could she even believe it possible that her father's trusted employee, Bill Cole, who would still, no doubt, have a key to the warehouse, would be working on his own.

In the yard, Sonya drew to a stop beside the squarish, old truck marked 'Brighton Furs', one of the delivery vans Bill Cole had for many years driven. Reluctantly, as if expecting to find it crammed with furs safely removed before the fire, she flashed the light into the cab. Then she circled the ancient vehicle, drew in her breath, and attempted to open the back door. It was stuck fast, but not locked. She made several more attempts before it came open.

The overhead racks held nothing, but the huge, hollow storage compartment, despite its total emptiness, still managed to look ominous.

Drawing away from the gleam of yard-light intensified Sonya's sense of isolation. She crossed the great length of weedy field, and at the entrance to the barn, her hand, shaking a little, hesitated on the ancient latch. When she gathered the nerve to open the door, strong scents of earth and straw drifted to her. The familiar smell steadied her, brought to mind a clear picture of Melvin LaVett, sunbrowned and smiling. The momentary calmness his image gave her faded quickly in the face of almost total blackness.

She circled the entire area, allowing the light to fall into corners and inside a car parked in the center. She climbed the crude, wooden steps near the doorway and flashed the light around the barren loft.

At last, fully satisfied that Uncle Alex had

not been staying with Bill Cole here at his farm, she started back to the car.

As she moved through the field, she felt an impression of eyes watching her. Her apprehension increased and so, too, did the speed of her steps.

Before she was able to reach her car, a voice from out of the darkness spoke.

"Sonya."

She whirled around.

A man emerged from the growth of trees beside the house. He approached with quick strides, drawing to a sudden stop and standing with his straight, military posture beneath the illumination of yard-light. Since she'd last seen Bill Cole, his features had grown thinner, sharper, more deeply-etched with lines. Despite the gray hair, he looked like some soldier on guard duty, one not afraid of night or danger.

He must have been alerted the moment she'd driven onto his property.

Is Alex watching, too?

Her gaze strayed from Cole and skirted through the darkness. She had the impression he'd seen her enter his house, open the back of the delivery truck, go inside the barn. If so, why had he allowed her to complete her search? In his unwavering gaze she read no answers.

"I was looking for Uncle Alex," she said, faltering a little under his unblinking scrutiny.

"You'll not find him out here."

"But you know where he is."

Bill Cole made no motion at all, not of eyes or of lips, which remained pressed into a thin, hard line. Bill Cole had always been close-mouthed. She saw little hope now of his telling her anything.

Still, she pressed.

"I know you're helping him, Bill. You've got to tell me where he is. I need to talk to him."

When he didn't answer, she went on.

"You know Alex trusts me. You know you can, too."

Cole's voice, steady and resolute, answered quietly, "Alex will get in touch with you."

"Why won't you let me know where I can find him?"

"Alex was here just a while ago. He took one of my cars and left just as darkness fell."

"What's he doing?"

"He's going to find out who's behind the arson. And he's got a big lead."

"I only wish I knew how to help him," Sonya said. Her gaze met his again, and knowing that pleading with him was useless, she started toward her car.

"Sonya."

Again the sharp-spoken word. It caused her to stop, to face him.

"I do have one message for you, a warning from Alex. Stay away from Dan Rathmell."

CHAPTER 11

Voices from the kitchen floated clearly to Sonya as she entered the darkened front room.

"I'm worried about Alma," Connie was saying. "She's been crying all evening. I just don't know what's wrong with her, and now she won't come down for supper."

Connie's exasperation disturbed Emil, increased his gruffness.

"You know she hasn't been right in the head for a long time."

"Now, Emil, that's just not fair. Sis is just different, that's all."

"She's so stubborn," he said, almost with hatred. "She won't change her mind about anything!"

"Something's bothering her, Emil. And I'd like to know what it is. I can't stand to have Sis avoid me the way she's started doing. Do you suppose . . . it has to do with Alex's being gone?"

A chair creaked.

"How would I know?" An intense pause followed Emil's words.

Connie went on speaking as if she'd not even wanted to hear Emil's answer. "I've always taken care of Sis, you know that, even when Tom and I were married."

A pause, and then she continued mournfully.

"I've worked hard to give her things. Things I wanted myself."

"I don't see how you can stand the way she's always latched on to you," Emil snapped. "Sometimes I believe you think more of Alma than you do of me."

Connie continued, still as if she hadn't even heard him. "I just don't know what to do. Alma's just not acting like herself at all."

The scrape of a chair against the floor sounded sharp and angry. "I'll just go up and get her."

Emil's towering form appeared at the doorway. The light spilling over from the kitchen emphasized the dark beginnings of a beard and created shadows across his face, giving the cold passiveness always present there a deeper, more terrifying dimension.

Emil halted when he saw Sonya. She could feel the wordless clash between them. He knew she'd overheard the talk between

Connie and him. He didn't speak, just bypassed her, and with secretive, agile grace proceeded up the stairs.

Sonya crossed to the kitchen, filled with the smoky aroma of grilling steaks. On the table set a platter stacked high with roasting ears.

"I'll just put on a plate for you," Connie said.

Rumpled locks of long hair partially hid her face, but Sonya could identify in the tired slope of her shoulders a strain and worry she had not believed Connie could manifest.

Sonya automatically pulled out the nearest chair and stood tightly gripping the high arch of deeply carved wood.

Soon Emil strode back into the room. Alma, like a helpless animal, followed.

"Sit right down here, Sis," Connie said, rushing to her side. "We've been waiting supper for you."

Alma cringed a little as she sank down at the table. Emil walked around Sonya and seated himself between his wife and Connie.

Sonya had perceived from the first the attraction Connie and Emil felt for one another. But Emil's realizing that she was aware of it now caused an increase in the already tense atmosphere. She was relieved when Connie broke the heavy silence.

"I cooked this corn tonight because it's your favorite," she said, passing the platter across Emil to Alma.

Everyone watched Alma fill her plate. She, looking trapped and terrified, kept her stare fastened on the roasting ear.

Connie spoke again, this time to Sonya.

"I haven't seen your cousin all afternoon. Where do you suppose she's gone?"

"No telling about Jody."

"Alex doesn't like her very well, does he, Sonya? I mean, everyone knows, he just thinks the world of you. If he were in serious trouble, it's clear to me, you'd be the one he'd call on."

The chair creaked as Alma awkwardly changed positions. Beneath the sharp furrows of her brow, the large, usually vacant eyes, clouded with worry, fastened on Connie.

"What's happened to Alex?" Her hushed voice became pleading. "Where is he, Connie? Is he all right? Will he come back?"

"We just don't know, Alma." Connie attempting to be patient, hurriedly went on, "I think it's just terrible that he just up and leaves without even a word to me. I've been under such a strain." She cast a quick glance at Alma. "It looks as if you, in particular, would want to help me."

Alma stared again at her plate.

"What will happen," she asked, "if Alex never, ever comes back again?"

Sonya drew in her breath.

What does Alma know or suspect?

Sonya became suddenly unsure of both Dan and Bill Cole.

What if the two of them are working together, both against Alex?

Connie, around Emil's stiffened form, peered at her sister.

"Now what do you mean by that?" she demanded.

Sonya's gaze drifted from Alma to Connie to Emil. Somehow Connie's bold stare disturbed her much less than did Emil's secretive glances or Alma's tragic eyes.

In the deathlike stillness, Sonya suddenly realized all three of them were now watching her. She felt a sudden increase in apprehension. She stirred uneasily, the way Alma had a short time ago. Ever since she could remember, Alex had occupied this large chair with the ornately carved arms.

Why did I choose to sit here, so far away from the three of them, huddled together at the other end of the table?

Her heart wrenched as she thought about Uncle Alex. Of course, Alex, as perceptive as he was, would've figured out immediately the relationship between Connie and Emil. How hard those months of recovery must have been for Alex, seated here, with the three of them lined up against him, waiting, like vultures, for him to die.

Lined up against him, exactly as they now seemed to be lined up against her.

The windows to Sonya's room received the full effects of the first rays of rising sun. Sonya, remaining in bed for a moment longer, still half-asleep, pictured Dan dripping with water, black hair tousled and wet. She smiled as she remembered the teasing sparkle in his dark eyes as he'd pulled her into his arms and kissed her.

Then reality hit her and with it, Bill Cole's warning.

She should have called Dan last night and canceled their plans. She no longer wanted Dan's company on her trip to Kansas City to check out Emil's alibi.

Six thirty.

She dressed hurriedly, then removed Alex's address book from behind the portrait over the fireplace. Sonya flipped through pages to where Alex had scribbled, without name or phone number beside it, 5674 W. Market Street.

She'd just written down the address and slipped it into her purse when a tap sounded on the door.

Dan wore a white shirt and black trousers, adding height and leanness to his frame.

" 'Home is the sailor'," he said softly. Even though he greeted her with a joke, no humor showed in his eyes or in the tight set of his lips.

Sonya glanced away from him, her gaze holding to the painting of his father. This morning she could clearly see the great resemblance between father and son — the same slight tilt of head, the same eyes, dark, and chillingly remote.

Over the years she'd found her Uncle Alex's advice to be sound and valid. She must heed his warning now. No doubt Alex had access to information she didn't possess, information that would incriminate Dan.

Although Dan waited by the door, Sonya could imagine him standing in front of the warehouse, the blaze of flames behind him. Across the great gulf that was widening between them, she heard herself saying, "Alex and I are in a good deal of trouble unless we find out who set the fire."

"You could be in much deeper trouble if you do find out," Dan replied, his tone sounding almost like a threat.

The stillness between them persisted a long time before Sonya spoke again.

"Emil was in Linnville Thursday night. We've got to prove he was lying when he told the sheriff he was in Kansas City."

"Even if you find out Emil did lie, what does that really mean? Emil knows he's a suspect. Being the type of person he is, the first thing he would do, guilty or not, is invent an alibi. He may even be looking ahead, thinking of what a position he would be in if Alex is found dead."

Sonya tried to shake off Dan's chilling words. "Have you talked to Bill Cole?"

"I've tried to," Dan said. "I went out there, but he ordered me off his land."

"Then Bill must be hiding Alex."

"Or he's involved in this fraud himself."

"I think Alex knows who's guilty," Sonya said. "He wants to be able to prove it before he shows up here again."

"If Alex is that frightened of . . . whoever it is . . . then you should be, too, Sonya. You should stay completely out of this."

Dan paced a few steps away. He stopped, one hand clutching the fireplace mantel, directly beneath the painting of his father.

"I'm asking you, Sonya, to let me go to Kansas City alone. I want you to leave everything entirely up to me!"

"No, I'm going to Kansas City today."

She opened the door into the hallway, adding, "It's not necessary that you go with me."

With a flash of anger, but without answering, Dan followed her down the stairway and outside.

"Let's take my car," he said.

With resignation she slipped in the passenger's seat. He didn't speak again until they were headed toward Kansas City. Then he cast a quick, sideways glance toward her.

"The only one who'd benefit from the fire besides you is Alex. And if Alex hired someone else to carry out his plans, it wouldn't be Emil Steelman. He hates Emil and the feeling's mutual."

"Emil might take things into his own hands because of Connie," Sonya answered. "He's very concerned about Alex's decision to sell out. Emil might think if Alex received insurance money, he'd take the house off the market, and they could continue living here and eventually end up with the place."

"A long shot."

"You know as well as I do how they all work together. Connie married Uncle Alex so the three of them could get their hands on his property, and they aren't going to let it slip out of their control without a struggle. I'm sure none of them know . . ." She caught herself just in time, before she said, *that my name's on the deed.*

Altering her words, she went on

"They wouldn't know the business was in debt, so they'd be counting on a huge cash settlement."

"Cash," Dan added, "that would go directly to Connie if Alex should die."

Their stillness, filled with the sounds of the interstate traffic, lingered.

"If Emil is willing to go that far," Dan said, "then I'm right. You have no business setting yourself up as a target."

They sped past miles of flat grassland. The morning sun radiated heat that reflected against the glaring pavement and added to Sonya's discomfort. The idea of Dan's helping her investigate, the safety she'd anticipated in having Dan beside her, had so quickly become sullied. She couldn't trust him, now, not with Alex's words ringing in her ears. Because she couldn't confide in him, this whole trip was going to be a dismal waste of time.

As the full skyline of the city came into view, Dan, as if he could read her mind, said less grudgingly, "Where should we go first?"

Sonya reached for her purse. "Let's look for Market Street."

"What address?"

"5674 West."

At that moment Dan unexpectedly turned off the thoroughfare on to a side street. He slowly circled the block and parked the car near the highway.

"What are you doing?"

"Checking," he said, intently watching the steady flow of traffic in front of them. "Ever since we left Linnville, I've had this feeling that we're being followed."

"I didn't see anyone," Sonya said, startled.

"Then it must just be a case of the nerves."

Dan remained watching for a long time. When he finally started driving again, he continued to glance in the rear-view mirror. They wound through a maze of side streets, and, at last, seeming to know exactly where he was going, he turned west on Market Street. Residences changed slowly into a dreary line of small businesses: 'Martin's Used Furniture', 'Broadwalk Café', 'D & L Pawn'.

"What exactly are we looking for?" he asked.

"I found an address in the house," Sonya said evasively. "I just wanted to go by there."

Dan soon swung the car beneath the tin

canopy of a vacated service station. The numbers over the office read 5674. The office was adjoined by a huge garage made of cement blocks. The boarded windows, the graffiti on the once-whitewashed walls, gave the building an air of total desertion.

"I know why he had this address written down," Dan said. "About a year ago, Alex had talked about going into business with Melvin LaVett. He was impressed with LaVett's mechanical ability and hoped to make a little money on some side venture. Anyway, before they had a chance to open, Alex had that stroke and that ended that."

Sonya quietly surveyed the empty station, then the surrounding area, made up of the same sort of dilapidated buildings.

"Obviously nothings going on here," Sonya said. "Let's see if we can locate Johnny Wilbur."

"Emil usually hangs around Mayfield Gym when he's in town," Dan replied. "That might be a good place to start."

The gym, only a matter of blocks from the abandoned Market Street service station, contrasted with the rundown surroundings, and managed despite its age to look modern and important. Dan, as he left her just inside the huge auditorium, said, "I'll inquire in the office and see if Johnny

Wilbur's here."

Sonya stepped around the random arrangement of metal chairs toward the two wrestlers working out in the ring. Neither of them she took to be Johnny Wilbur, yet she felt drawn, as though hypnotized, to watch, and as she did, she began to feel shaken and deeply frightened.

Why she felt that way soon dawned upon her. In the brutish, bulging frame of the heavier of the men, in his circling, cautious motions, his quick contact and savage physical force, she was seeing Emil Steelman. This wrestler, who reminded her of Emil, held the other in a headlock, which no amount of wrenching and struggling loosened. The two crashed to the floor, the lighter man flopping helplessly and moaning aloud. The other man's face, like Emil's, remained impassively cruel.

A voice startled her.

"You got an interest in the kid?"

Sonya turned to a thin man in a shabby, business suit, who, as he talked, continued to write on a small pad.

"I'm trying to locate Johnny Wilbur."

The long, bony face smiled sarcastically.

"Try Falcum Boarding House, just a block south. Old Johnny, he gets out of bed later and later these days."

"Was he here Thursday night?"

The man brought the tip of the ballpoint to his lips.

"Thursday? No. Johnny generally hangs around here only on week ends. I haven't seen anything of him since last Sunday."

"Has Emil Steelman been here?"

"Emil Steelman." He repeated the name with admiration. "Emil Steelman! You mean Mr. Satan! Now, there's a real winner for you!" He wrote in his note-pad again. "Steelman used to try to train Johnny, but I figure he's given up on him. They haven't practiced here for several months."

"They were supposed to be training Thursday night. You didn't see either of them? Were you here all evening?"

"I'm always here, lady. I manage the place." He wandered off, still scribbling.

Sonya glimpsed Dan coming out of the office. As she joined him, he said, "I've got Wilbur's apartment number."

The words 'Falcum Boarding House' stood out on the sad old building in huge amateurish lettering. Dan and Sonya entered a careworn lobby set about with old card tables and folding chairs. Two elderly men lounged on a squalid couch watching some sports event on TV.

Dan approached and asked, "Is Johnny around?"

"He just left a while ago," the younger of the two answered.

"He was supposed to have met me here Thursday evening," Dan said. "I was here at nine o'clock, but he wasn't."

The two men looked at each other.

"Thursday we were all present and accounted for. That's our poker night. Sure didn't see you, though."

"Did Wilbur play poker with you all evening?"

"We sat right over there," the older man replied, indicating the tables with a sweep of a veined hand. "Johnny lost game after game. We quit right after midnight."

"Was Emil Steelman playing cards, too?" Sonya asked.

"I know Emil Steelman," the other man answered. "Used to watch him down at Mayfield Gym. But, no, I haven't seen Emil in a very long time."

"Well, ain't that funny?" the older man cut in, leaning forward to peer around Dan and Sonya. "There's Emil Steelman coming in right now."

Emil moved toward them with quick, cat-like steps, leaving his companion, a heavy-framed, coarse-featured man wearing smudged, gray sweats, standing near the door.

He drew to a sudden stop. His eyes, filled with disdain, switched with eerie slowness from Dan to Sonya.

Sonya was aware of Dan's stepping forward, so he, not Sonya, would be the one directly facing the man. She felt a moment of gratitude for the solid wall Dan made between them.

"Speak of the devil." The older of the two men behind Sonya gave a brittle laugh. "Mr. Satan, in the flesh!"

Emil, ignoring the remark, looked over his shoulder toward the doorway.

"Johnny," he drawled. "This is old man Brighton's stepson. And his niece."

The beginning of a smile died, and Johnny's mouth tightened over yellowish teeth. For a moment he appeared hopelessly lost. Then he spoke, in coughing, tortured voice.

"What are they doing here? What do they want?"

Sonya's gaze left Johnny Wilbur and raised to Emil's brutal face.

The stillness in the room held a challenge — a challenge they both recognized and accepted.

"I want to know," Sonya said, "where you

really were the night the warehouse fire was set."

"Don't ask me that." Cold fury settled over Emil. He jerked his head toward Dan. "Ask him." He turned to confront Dan, his voice edged with contempt. "No one knows more about that fire than you do."

CHAPTER 12

The door to Sonya's room opened and Alma, without having bothered to knock or call out, trudged inside. She sounded miserable.

"No one's home. Would you care if I stayed with you for a while?"

"Not at all," Sonya said.

"I won't bother you." A hopeful smile struggled with Alma's blank expression. "I'll just sit over here."

She settled herself into a nearby chair. For some reason she was carrying a paper sack. "I'll be just as quiet as a mouse."

Sonya had to ask.

"Where's Connie and Emil?"

"They didn't tell me where they were going," Alma replied mournfully. "It's scary here all alone."

She sorted through the sack.

"I'm going to give you this," she said, extending a print apron. "I made it for

Connie, but I'm going to give it to you."

Sonya accepted the gift, an apron checked with brilliant patches of red and blue.

"Thank you, Alma. It's very beautiful."

Alma's attention, straying away from Sonya, centered on John T. Rathmell's portrait.

"Why is he so sad?"

"He doesn't look all that sad to me. See, he's smiling."

As Sonya spoke, she couldn't help shrinking a little from John T. Rathmell's expression — the way it hinted of some secret deceit.

"No, he's very sad," Alma insisted stubbornly. "What makes him sad? Is he sad because he did something wrong?"

"What do you think he did wrong?"

"I don't know. There's so many things a person can do. It's wrong to hurt people, to tell lies, and to . . ."

Alma's words stopped suddenly, causing Sonya to prompt.

"To what?"

"To set fires."

Rows of lines cut deeply into Alma's forehead, giving her entire face an overtone of tragedy. Was she worried, Sonya asked herself suddenly, because she knew that Connie and Emil had plotted the arson?

"Do you have any idea who set fire to the warehouse?"

Alma shrank deeper into the chair. Her voice took on an introspective tone as she answered. "Grandma always told me not to hurt anyone. Grandma raised Connie and me." Her voice grew prideful.

"Grandma left all her money to me, not Connie. 'Connie can take care of herself,' Grandma said, 'but I want you to always have something just for you.' "

Alma's childlike ramblings had begun to engage Sonya's pity. No doubt Connie had married young, and Emil had probably taken up with Alma in order to be near Connie. She thought of Alma's pathetic adoration of Connie with a little shudder.

What a position to be in — caught between Connie's hypocrisy and Emil's cruelty.

"Connie's so smart," Alma said, in the same worshipful tone she'd just used in speaking of her grandmother. "She's pretty, too, isn't she?"

"Yes. Did Connie tell you when they'd be back?"

"No, but they left together a long time ago."

Alma got quickly to her feet.

"I think I'd better get back downstairs. They wouldn't like it if they knew I was up

162

here talking to you."

When Alma wandered off, Sonya's thoughts eventually turned to her cousin Jody. No use putting it off, Sonya needed to see George Malroy right away and pay off Jody's bad check.

She rose wearily and went downstairs. Connie and Emil had returned, but only Connie occupied the front room. She, looking very agitated, stood staring out of the front window.

"Is Jody back?" Sonya inquired.

"She's not staying here any longer; I set her straight on that. Not in my house. Not after the way she talked to me."

"Jody doesn't mean everything she says."

"I just told her to flat get out," Connie returned belligerently. " 'You're never, ever, to come around here again,' I said. 'I don't mind Sonya, but you don't need to think I'm putting up with you.' "

"What did Jody say to make you so angry?"

Again Connie's lips compressed.

"No one's ever talked to me like that. She said I'd married Alex just so I could get my hands on his money."

Connie stopped, indignantly drawing in her breath. "Then, of all things, she accused me of killing him! Can you believe that? After all I've done for Alex!"

Inside Malroy's Cafe, a loud country song blared from a stereo, and a crowd of people laughed and talked. Often the place was filled with dancers, especially on Saturday night when George Malroy hired live music. Although everything else had changed for Sonya, nothing at all had changed at Malroy's. The whitewashed walls were still decorated with faded posters of country singers, and the floor was a casual disarray of tables.

The owner, a heavy-set man everyone simply referred to as Malroy, leaned on the cash register reading a newspaper. He looked up as she approached.

"Sonya! What a surprise!" he exclaimed, stepping forward and crushing her in a hug. "And they say only bad pennies return."

Malroy, although his long hair and beard had grayed, still seemed young because of a vibrant ever-present exuberance. He was always surrounded by a following, people with no particular correlation of age or status.

With his arm around her, Malroy led her toward the counter. The old buckskin shirt with long fringes and the unkempt beard made him look like a mountain man from long ago.

"What a very long time. I hear about how successful you are, traveling all over the world. Hope you're back in Linnville for good."

"Probably not."

"Dan comes in all the time. He's always talking about you, telling me where you are and what you say in your letters."

Sonya didn't want to go there.

"Have you seen Alex?"

Malroy ran a hand across the grizzly beard.

"Sorry to say, no. I haven't seen hide or hair of him since the trouble with the warehouse."

Dan had told her Malroy had seen Uncle Alex and Bill Cole together that night after the fire. Clearly one of them wasn't telling her the truth. The possibility that it might be Dan left her feeling stunned.

"What about Bill Cole?"

"Haven't seen Bill either, not for several months."

"Not even driving by?"

"No."

"But Dan's been here."

"Nope. Haven't seen him for several days now."

Malroy returned her long, skeptical gaze with his bold, unflinching one. If Malroy had decided to remain silent concerning Alex, he wasn't going to change his mind no matter how much she questioned him.

"I've really come here to ask you about Jody," she said at last.

"That one," Malroy fumed, "I wish I hadn't seen! She wrote me a three hundred dollar no-funder!"

Sonya could see indignation building up in him as he spoke of Jody.

"I don't mind helping people, but there's no helping that little gal. It's just like I told her the other night, if I don't get the money by this Monday, I'm turning the check over to the county attorney."

Jody had mentioned the sum of two hundred dollars, but Sonya was used to her cousin's unreliable facts.

"May I take a look at the check?"

Malroy walked to the cash register and angrily tapped a key. From under a thick stack of bills he produced Jody's check. Sonya studied the giant capital letters followed by that characteristic, almost unreadable line. 'Jody Porter'. Jody had mentioned she was using her maiden name again.

"It's dated back in March," Sonya said,

surprised, "and this is almost the end of May."

"That doesn't matter; I can still turn it over. I've been patient, trying to give her time to pick it up."

"How long has Jody been in town?"

"I first saw her in December. I remember, it was right before Christmas. Jody had that mistletoe in her hair and was trying to get everyone to kiss her. You know how she always clowns around."

As he spoke, he took the check back with a quick movement and replaced it in the cash register.

"When you see Jody, tell her that old man Malroy isn't going to hold the bag for no bad check."

"Do you have any idea where I might find her?" Sonya asked.

"If I were looking for her, I'd try the state lake. You know how she loves to camp."

"I'm going to pick up this check," Sonya said, taking out her checkbook, "but only this one."

"Don't think I'm fool enough to do any more business with Jody."

Malroy watched in silence as if he wasn't going to risk her being distracted from her task. He accepted the new check.

"The sheriff knows I'm Alex's friend," he

offered. "He's been in several times asking about him."

Sonya busied herself tucking her checkbook away.

"But you don't have any idea where Alex might be?"

"No, but if you hear anything, you let me know."

Which was exactly what she wanted to say to him.

Sonya left Malroy's, a sick feeling starting in the pit of her stomach. Jody had been in Linnville since Christmas. December was the month Alex had spent in bed recovering from the stroke — the month he'd been robbed of all of Anna's personal effects.

She took a different route from town, following the old road flanking the rear of the Brighton land, one tracking past Alex's barn and by the old Bailey place. Eventually she would end up at the state lake where Malroy had told her Jody would probably be staying.

The air from the wide-open windows had grown still and oppressive. At first, Sonya had thought the haze that had fallen over the road ahead was caused from layers of heat emanating from the blacktop. Then, suddenly she smelled the strong, unmistakable odor of smoke.

She leaned forward, straining to make out the image of Alex's barn through the thick gray-black cloud that had formed just ahead of her. She jammed her foot down on the brake, and the car skidded to a stop. Flames overran the west side of the old wooden frame and had begun leaping through the roof.

Sonya made a sharp u-turn and sped back toward the Brighton turnoff. The car lunged forward on the hard-packed dirt road, bumping and jolting, toward the barn.

Panic gripped her long before she reached the massive old building, long before her car had skidded to a stop a safe distance from the open door.

Horrified, Sonya watched as angry flames lapped across the front side of the barn, casting a sinister glow across the peeling red paint. She stared at the inferno, aghast, just as she had at the warehouse. No matter how fast she acted now, she wouldn't be able to save it — the old landmark would soon collapse in total ruin.

As she watched, appalled, Sonya was all but overcome by a sudden realization, one as all-consuming as the raging flames. This fire was no accident — it had been deliberately set, just like the arson at Brighton's Furs.

She started to back away, to go after help. But before she could reach her car, a piercing sound came from inside the barn, rising shrilly above the crackling of flames.

Could that noise be caused by metal crashing against metal?

The screech assaulted her ears again. Sonya whirled around. Her heart seemed to stop. It was a terrified wail, a human cry made by someone trapped inside the barn.

CHAPTER 13

Could Sonya bring herself to enter the burning building, come face to face with a another fire? Feeling choked by self-doubt, she nevertheless sprang forward through the entrance.

She halted there, heart pounding, her eyes straining to see through the rolling smoke. Flames, leaping high, raged through the bales of hay along the west wall. In no time at all the entire barn would be engulfed by fire!

Sonya located the figure sprawled beneath the ladder leading to the loft. She could distinguish nothing save a dim outline. Fingers of fire spurted and crackled very close to the still form.

Would risking her own life be of any use? Whoever lay there was probably already beyond rescue! She thought of going on to Dan's cabin and calling for help, but she knew there would be no hope of saving the person inside if she left. She backed away, then stopped. How could she allow this already out-of-control fire to consume a human life and do nothing?

Sonya sucked in one last deep breath of fresh air, then with attention fixed on the ladder, she began to move steadily across the vast distance separating her from the body.

She raised her cotton blouse to cover her face, but in spite of the shield, thick smoke began at once to cause spasms of uncontrollable coughing. She estimated that she'd reached the center of the barn, but, while standing up she could no longer recognize shapes and forms. She sank to the ground and on hands and knees, edged forward.

Sonya had hoped that she'd be able to lift the person, but when she recognized Alma's bulky figure, the possibility faded. She turned the woman's face toward her. She couldn't make out her features because of the reaction of smoke in her eyes. But she could feel blood on her hands, was aware of the pool of it on the dirt floor.

A moan escaped Sonya's lips as she struggled with the deadweight of Alma's body. The flames had reached the loft, had already began to engulf the roof. Would she be able to get Alma outside before becoming overcome by smoke? Was Alma dead anyway?

Not knowing, Sonya began to drag Alma away from the flames that would in a short minute or two encircle her. She worked with a persistent determination, rejecting the weakness in her limbs and the inward cry telling her to abandon this hopeless task and save herself.

Alma's cumbersome form seemed an active force resisting all the energy Sonya could muster. Seized again with coughing, she was forced to stop. She told herself she was headed in the right direction and was making progress. She could with great effort still make out the faint, blurred image of the open door, but it seemed to grow farther away as she edged forward.

Once more Sonya halted, gasping for breath. When she started on again, an almost unbearable pressure filled her lungs. In spite of it, she kept tugging at Alma, inching her forward until she could do so no longer. She slumped forward and covered her face with her hands, praying, as she did, that she'd find the strength to continue.

When she looked up again, she felt totally lost. Where was the doorway? She felt incapable of seeing, of moving. She was going to die here in this barn with Alma.

Heat, so intense she felt she was burning up, bit at her. As if totally blindfolded, having no sense of direction, she attempted again to drag Alma with her. The imminence of death gave her new power, made it possible to resist the pain that had spread from her chest throughout her entire body.

During the long period of time filled with what seemed like minute, undirected activity, she thought of Dan. If only they had the chance to marry, to make a life together, to be happy. Why hadn't she told him she loved him when she'd been given the chance? Now he would never know for sure just how very much she cared for him.

Sonya stopped again and tried to see through the smoke.

Is that daylight just ahead or merely reflections of firelight?

Straining, she made out the faint outline of a door, one that seemed an endless distance away. Was it possible that she could keep on moving Alma toward it?

She felt a prompting to leave her burden and try to escape alone. It was clear she could save herself if she abandoned Alma. But she knew she could never leave her, for Alma might still be alive.

Just above her, boards broke lose from the floor of the loft and crashed, burning, beside them. Fiercely now, Sonya renewed her struggling. Little by little they came closer to the doorway.

Not stopping her activity even when she was outside, she continued dragging Alma away from the burning structure.

After the fits of coughing were past, Sonya looked toward Alma's motionless form. Her build was short and stocky compared to Connie's, but her face, gray as ashes, bore some resemblance to her sister's.

The gash across the side of her head looked wide-open and deep. Sonya ripped Alma's blouse and pressed the material, flowered like the apron she'd given Sonya, tightly against it to stop the flow of blood. Was she breathing? Sonya leaned closer but couldn't tell.

She lifted one of Alma's eyelids. The pupil looked strangely large. Why had she been struck down with such brutality? The thought came to her as a question, but Sonya was certain of the answer. Alma had somehow found out who had robbed Alex and burned the warehouse. That's what had caused the sudden change in her behavior. When Alma had come into her room, Sonya should have tried harder to find out exactly how much Alma knew — the knowledge that had led to this!

How could anyone be so cold-blooded? What could the thief expect to gain that would merit killing poor Alma?

Aware that she was crying now, Sonya groped for Alma's wrist and tried to feel for a pulse, but the excited pounding of her own heartbeat left her incapable of drawing any conclusions.

Soon the fire would be spotted, she told herself. Someone would summon help. She glanced fearfully toward the barn, enclosed now in a frightening yellow-red blaze. Little trails of fire licked through the dry, surrounding grass.

Sonya rose and looked down at Alma. Blood, soaking through the makeshift bandage, escaped and flowed down across the tapering line of her face. Her eyelids remained closed and still. Sonya detected not the slightest movement of chest to indicate breath. If Alma were still alive, Sonya had not a moment to spare!

Gasping, she stumbled backward, then whirled and began running toward Dan's cabin, which set just over the rise of the hill. She raced through the high growth of underbrush and into the trees covering the steep slope. At the summit, she spotted Dan. He was standing, unmoving, alertly observing, listening. In no time his gaze came to rest on her.

Had he, drawn by the smoke, just left his cabin to investigate? Or had he been up here all along watching as Alex's barn became an inferno?

Sonya drew to a halt. Her hand reached out to clutch at a nearby branch for support. Pain burned through her lungs with each intake of breath.

Dan moved rapidly, feet sliding against rocks, toward her. Waves of nausea threatened her, and Dan's image became blotched with blackness.

He gathered her into his arms.

In spite of her doubts and suspicions, she buried her head against his shoulder. When she managed to look up at him, she half-expected to see a reflection of leaping flames glowing in the blackness of his eyes.

"What's happened, Sonya?"

"Someone set fire to the barn. Alma was inside."

A sob broke through her words.

"I managed to get her out, but she may be dead!"

"You go back and stay with her. I'll call for help and be with you as fast as I can!"

Her entire body shaking, Sonya retraced her course down the slope, back across the field. She slumped to the ground beside Alma's motionless form. Immense heat, the terrible smell of smoke and ashes, settled solidly around her.

She waited for what seemed like hours, holding a bandage she'd made from her own blouse to Alma's head. She'd lost so much blood. And the wound continued to bleed.

Sonya didn't hear Dan's approach, but she became aware of his bending over her.

"Let me take a look."

Gratefully, sliding back out of his way, she relinquished her station. Through hazy layers of smoke, she watched Dan open Alma's eyelid, the way she had done, then examine the deep gash. His sharp frown, the shadow that had moved into his eyes, confirmed her worst fears. He spoke, in a mystified tone.

"Why would anyone want to harm her? She never hurt anyone. She was . . ."

His voice trailed off but the word 'was' lingered around them both. Sonya found herself too choked with tears to give any answer.

At last, the shrillness of a siren broke through the sputtering and snap of burning wood. Relief flooded over Sonya as the ambulance arrived, and white-coated attendants hurried toward them. Their arrival was soon followed by a series of fire trucks, of men, quick and organized, like an invading army.

As the paramedics bent over Alma, Dan inquired about her condition.

"Concussion and severe burns," the older of the two replied. "We'll get this oxygen operating, then rush her to the emergency room."

Sonya, Dan's arm supporting her, watched as the paramedics worked with Alma, as they strapped her to a stretcher. They followed along as they placed her inside the ambulance.

Dan looked silently after the vehicle as it bumped across the uneven ground toward the highway.

"I wish I knew what was going on here," he said grimly, as if to himself. Then he turned to Sonya and drew her into his arms. He held her close for a moment, then spoke.

"It looks as if I'll have to follow you every minute to keep you safe."

CHAPTER 14

Sonya had left the hospital hours ago, and now, shaken and exhausted, she waited expectantly for Connie to return with some news of Alma.

Shadows fell across the front room and added to the darkness of her thoughts. What had started out as a crime against property had magnified, had become tragedy, maybe even murder.

Alex had been right. His life was in danger, and, even though Alex wasn't aware of it, so, too, was hers. From the violent attack on the child-like Alma, Sonya knew they faced a pitiless enemy.

After a long time had passed, a car pulled into the driveway. Connie, head bent, assisted by both Emil and Melvin LaVett, started toward the house. Gloom, like a black funnel cloud, followed their slow progress up the porch steps toward the door.

Sonya's heart sank. Alma must have died.

Once inside, Connie sank down on the rocker. She buried her face in her hands and wept. Emil towered above her. For the first time since Sonya had met him, he looked ineffective, unsure.

Sonya glanced toward Melvin, standing tall and straight by the door. Although his eyes met hers, she read no message in them and was forced to ask.

"How is Alma?"

She could tell the answer wasn't going to be good by the tense tightening of his lips.

"She hasn't regained consciousness yet."

Connie's sobbing became louder. Emil, bending over her, spoke gruffly.

"I can't stand to hear you carrying on like this. Will you try to stop? Get control of yourself. For my sake if not for yours."

"No one knows what's going to happen, Connie," Melvin added in a kind, supportive way. "Alma may surprise us all and come out of this."

His consoling words brought only a low wail of pain.

"You know she's never going to wake up!"

She gripped Emil's shirt-sleeve imploringly, tears making little trails across her face as she sobbed out her self-recriminations.

"I've always been able to protect her. Why

181

didn't I try harder? Why did I let her down just when she needed me most?"

Emil wouldn't allow Connie to blame herself.

"You did everything you could to find out what was wrong with her. It wasn't your fault that Alma refused to tell you."

It wasn't enough to settle Connie.

"Why wouldn't she tell me? You know how close Alma and I are."

Her words broke off, then began again, increasing in volume.

"All my life it's been Alma and me, trying to get along the best we could. What will I ever do without her?"

Emil patted her shoulder. The gentle gesture somehow seemed ill-timed, out of character, and awkward.

"Let me get you a cup of coffee," he said, as if coffee had power to dissolve her grief. But still she wailed.

"Who could have done this, Emil? Why would anyone harm her? Alma was always so very kind, never hurt anyone or anything!"

"You try to settle down." Emil patted her shoulder again and headed for the kitchen as if he would find there a solution to his problems.

Connie's head dropped back to her hands.

Strings of black hair scattered through clutching fingers. Her voice was muffled as she asked, "Has Henry been here?"

Sonya thought of the sheriff and felt grateful that he hadn't chosen to question her tonight.

"No, not yet."

"He was at the hospital," Connie said, both hands still pressed against her face.

"He acted like he was suspicious of you, Sonya. I just don't understand that. I told him if you'd been the one who had hit Alma, you'd have just left her in the barn to burn up. But he didn't seem to think so."

"I don't know why he would suspect me," Sonya said tiredly.

"Whatever happens, I know you tried to save her, Sonya," Connie said, her voice choked with tears. "I'll always be thankful to you for that."

After a while, Connie burst out indignantly, "If I were you, I'd get right on the phone and have it out with Henry here and now."

Melvin rejoined the conversation.

"He's just doing his job, trying to find out what's behind all of this." As he spoke, he crossed the room and seated himself beside Sonya.

"And if anyone knows the answer to that,

it's Alex," he told her earnestly. "If you know where he is, Sonya, you'd better tell the sheriff."

"I don't know where he is."

"The sheriff was headed out here, but I told him that you were in no shape to answer any questions tonight."

As Melvin spoke, lean, sun-browned fingers tightening protectively around hers. He leaned towards her.

"Why don't you go on upstairs, Sonya, and get some rest? I'm just going to stay here tonight in case I'm needed."

She was too tired to answer, to care.

The perking of coffee from the kitchen sounded loud in the stillness. Soon Connie's low, plaintive sobbing started again.

Emil appeared, carrying a large mug. He pushed it at Connie.

"Here. Drink this."

Connie accepted the cup, holding it motionlessly in her hands.

Emil stood very straight, muscles budging in his thick neck. He slanted a secretive glance toward Sonya as he might have done to an opponent in a wrestling bout.

"When you were helping Alma, did she say anything to you?"

Emil's demanding tone caused a reaction of fear in Sonya, one that prompted visions to arise in her mind. She saw Alma fleeing from the house, and Emil, with deadly slowness, following her to the barn. There, in confrontation, Alma informed him she was going to tell all she knew. Sonya could picture Emil's powerful hand wielding the blow, and she could see him lighting the fire.

His harsh voice cut into her terrifying thoughts.

"Was Alma ever conscious? I want to know!"

Reacting to the hostility present in his words, Sonya met his gaze in silence.

Emil's manner became more insistent.

"Just what did Alma tell you?"

"Nothing." Sonya rose.

"I'm very tired. I'm going up to bed."

She could feel Emil's gaze on her back as she walked out.

Hatred.

Alma had lived through the night, but the prognosis on her condition remained hopelessly bleak. To top it all off, Connie informed Sonya that the sheriff had arrived early and was waiting for her in Alex's study.

The feeling of complete physical weakness returned and caused a shaking in her legs. Sonya paused to collect herself before she

185

opened the door.

She'd always considered the sheriff an approachable man of no stern demands or great will, but when she entered the room, that impression lost all validity. Davis' narrowed gray eyes, the thoughtful sag to his mouth, made him appear harsh and exacting. He seemed to have passed some final judgment upon her.

To her surprise he didn't begin questioning her about the fire. Instead he said, "I want you to look around this room."

Sonya scanned the row after row of books lining the shelves, but didn't note anything unusual. She wandered around, pausing before a picture hanging over one of the cases, puzzled about what he was expecting her to see.

"Carefully, Miss Brighton. Examine that print. No, the one of Roosevelt."

Sonya faced the smiling photograph of F.D.R., and after a careful appraisal, noticed what Henry Davis was referring to — the picture had been taken apart, the reframing very carelessly done.

"Now come over to the desk."

She complied, feeling like a puppet he could jostle about at will.

The sheriff opened the top drawer, then, with increasing pace, the second, halting before the third and last, the one Alex always kept locked. The padlock was still clamped in place but the hasp had been pried off.

"Someone broke into this desk. Do you know what Mr. Brighton kept in this drawer?"

"That's where he kept his revolver, a Smith and Wesson 22."

"That's what Mrs. Brighton told me."

When Davis looked at her, an accusation flared across his heavy features and continued, like the fire she had battled, to smolder.

"Everything in this library has been searched since the last time I was in here. I'm sure you can see for yourself, absolutely nothing has been left untouched. I thought you might be able to tell me why."

He bore down on the word 'why', watching her closely.

Sonya faltered before the great forcefulness. She hadn't realized he possessed it.

"Someone might be looking for my uncle's will," she suggested.

"Miss Brighton, you and I both know Alex Brighton no longer has anything of significance to leave."

"Quite so. Other people might not know that." She hesitated, then added, "Or they could have been searching for cash."

"For what purpose, do you suppose, would your uncle hide money?"

Again, Sonya knew what he was thinking — payoff money for the arson.

"I'm not saying he did, only that someone could have thought so."

The sheriff's harsh gaze followed her as she stepped away.

"Did you search this room?"

He bit the words out, almost as if he was contemptuous of her.

"I did not."

Davis' eyes, as if to intimidate her, continued to bore into hers.

"You can admit it. It means nothing except that you knew your uncle had in his possession something worth finding."

"It means nothing? I resent very much what it means. I'm not in the habit of taking things that don't belong to me."

The sheriff leaned back in the swivel chair. He folded his hands across his wide expanse of stomach and spoke slowly.

"We don't all love our uncles, Miss Brighton. But we do all love money. It's nothing to be ashamed of."

Her face felt seared again, as it had when she'd battled the flames overtaking the barn.

"Whatever you think, why don't you just say it directly?"

"All right. I believe everything that's been happening here is connected with the warehouse arson . . . even the attempt made on Alma Steelman's life."

"Why do you think I would try to kill Alma, then try to save her?"

"You didn't try to kill her. Your partner did."

"And who is that?"

"Your uncle, of course. Where is he?"

"Uncle Alex would never harm anyone."

Tears formed in Sonya's eyes.

"For all I know, someone may have murdered him."

Davis ignored her words.

"Brighton can't hide out forever," he assured her, then added coldly, "I'm sorry you're not cooperating with me. You might very well find yourself an accessory to murder."

CHAPTER 15

What had the person who had searched Alex's study expected to find? Sonya was faced with the horrible possibility that the sheriff might have been right all along, that the intruder was looking for cash. Alex could have gotten a hold of enough money to hire someone to commit the warehouse arson. Then, when the job was bungled, and Alex was being blamed for the crime, he'd refused to make the final payment. Afraid of whoever he'd hired, Alex had simply left and the arsonist was now taking things into his own hands.

No!

Sonya couldn't believe Alex was guilty. This was more likely the work of the same thief who had invaded Alex's home when he had taken ill right before Christmas. The person had been bold enough to sneak into her uncle's house and carry off everything of value he could get his hands on.

In her mind, first Jody's face, then Dan's, alternated with frightening rapidity as that of the unknown burglar. Robber and . . . maybe even killer — a shiver ran through her as she debated on what she should do next.

It seemed to Sonya that the searcher had been hunting for cash or for some papers, maybe a will, that he might find hidden behind something as flat as a picture frame. Sonya believed he'd taken Alex's revolver only as an afterthought, that he'd entered the study for an entirely different purpose.

She was certain the searcher hadn't found what he'd wanted. Uncle Alex would never hide anything he considered of value in such an accessible location, rather in some out-of-the-way spot. *The third-floor landing!*

Sonya headed up to the old ballroom, which in recent years was seldom-used — where in the early 1900's the Rathmell family had thrown their extravagant parties.

For many years, despite the reclusive life Alex and Anna led, Anna had kept the vast room in glorious repair, polished the oak floors and quality furniture, papered the walls in shades of velvet red and black.

Now, glaring light from shadeless windows cast an unreal brilliance over an open area. The elaborate furnishings had been removed. All that was left was Alex's battered trunk and several stacks of pictures leaning against the wall behind it.

Sonya knelt, opened the trunk, and began rummaging through Alex's belongings — ordinary keepsakes, his army uniform, a bayonet, papers held together with rubber bands. She shuffled through them, a few she paused to read. An honorable discharge, a citation for bravery, love letters from Anna.

Assailed by the heavy scent of mothballs, she shook out Alex's army uniform and began looking through the pockets. To her disappointment, she found nothing.

Was there any use continuing her search? Where else would Alex think to hide something he wanted no one else to find?

"Sonya. Just what are you doing up here?"

Connie's voice, the bold ring now so familiar to her, caused Sonya to close the trunk and rise.

"I just wanted to take a look at the ball-room," Sonya said. "I haven't been in this section of the house for many years."

"Someone was looking around Alex's study, too." Connie's lips drew together tightly, but she didn't turn her statement into an accusation. Instead, almost defensively, she explained, "I came upstairs hunting for you and saw the door to the third

192

floor wide open."

"Is there news about Alma?"

"I called a couple of times during the night, but there wasn't any change. That's where I'm going now, to the hospital."

"Why do you think Alma was attacked?" Sonya asked.

"I think someone's just plumb crazy."

"Maybe not. Maybe Alma knows something that's put her life in danger."

"She did act . . . different before this happened," Connie answered thoughtfully, "You may be right."

"It wouldn't hurt to talk to the sheriff about protecting her now. They could post a guard at the hospital."

"I never thought of that. Yes, that's exactly what we need to do."

Immediately, Connie started away but drew to a sudden stop, as if just remembering why she'd been looking for Sonya.

"I came up here to tell you that Jody stopped by to see you. You should have seen the way she acted when I refused to let her in. To tell you the truth, Sonya, I'm half afraid of her."

"Jody has a flair for saying and doing all the wrong things. Deep down, she's not all that bad."

"I hope not. I think it's up to you to talk

to her, Sonya. Just tell her, no matter what she's up to, she's not to be on this property again."

Other reasons existed for Sonya's need to have a talk with Jody. Instead of letting Sonya know she'd been in the area for many months, Jody had gone out of her way to make it appear as if she'd just arrived in Linnville. Under different circumstances, considering Jody's usual carelessness, Sonya would've thought little about it, but at this time, Jody's lack of speaking up seemed outright deceit.

While Sonya had been inside continuing her search of the house, a cloudburst had arisen and had just as suddenly abated. Thick clouds now covered the sky, casting a gloomy darkness across the fields. Sonya drove slowly, watching for the old, wooden sign that would read, 'Baxter County Lake, Five Miles'.

Sonya remembered when she and Dan had driven to Kansas City, and Dan had thought someone was trailing them. She was gripped by that very same feeling now. Twice she slowed and waited for vehicles to draw nearer, only to be passed by a semi-truck, and a farmer in a pickup.

She pulled off the road a third time, and

unable to see traffic from any direction, she became satisfied she was utterly alone.

Jody surely must be out at the lake. Very few other places existed for someone without funds. Sonya began to feel a little sorry about their last meeting. She'd been pressured by her own troubles and impatient and irritated over Jody's total lack of responsibility. She should have been more understanding and made an effort to talk over Jody's problems with her.

When she'd heard about Jody's fight with Connie, she shouldn't have postponed looking for her and at least loaned Jody enough money to rent a motel. Now she would make an attempt to restore their old relationship, which, if not affectionate, had at least been friendly.

Sonya had, after all, never turned down any of Jody's quite frequent requests for help. A heaviness of unwanted duty hung over her, and she tried to replace it with thoughts of the two of them as girls, hanging out together at Linnville High.

Sonya spotted the sign. She steered the car from the blacktop onto a dirt road where in places water had cut deep gullies. The vehicle jogged slowly around curves overhung with branches.

The circumstance of Jody being in town

at the time Alex was robbed didn't neces-
sarily mean she was guilty of the crime. Jody
would, of course, put off the unpleasant task
of visiting the sick. She could merely have
hung around town doing just what Jody
always managed to do — have fun, be irresponsible — forgetting all about Uncle
Alex and his sorrows. Emil, whose entire
life seemed to have been an effort to grab
money and glory, and not his by rights, was
much more likely than Jody to resort to
stealing. Sonya decided she'd try not to assume Jody was guilty of everything because
she was guilty of a few indiscretions.

The sudden presence of thick trees made
the isolated park area darker, totally separated from the outside world. From the
open window, frogs and locusts sounded,
but, at the same time, the park managed to
seem engulfed in eerie stillness.

Jody's old white van was angled toward a
sagging picnic table close to the water.
Flames from a campfire leaped high into
the air as if protesting the sudden sallies of
wind. The uncertain flare of fire brought
back memories of the burning warehouse,
of the flames enclosing the barn, of Alma.

Through the storm-filled dimness Sonya
could see the scattering of empty tables, but
she saw no vehicles except for Jody's van.

Slightly nauseated by the strong odor of smoke, she left the car, veered around boxes and clutter scattered on the ground, and looked into the van, whose side door had been flung open. A suitcase lay flat on the floor. An empty cot was covered with a ruffled sleeping bag. But no sign of Jody.

Her anger toward Jody vanished suddenly, and she became anxious. Why had she allowed Jody to leave the house with nowhere to go? No telling what might happen to her alone in a place like this.

She moved toward the picnic table. A half-filled pan of chili and a pot of coffee set upon the camp stove. Both were cold. Two cups and two bowls lay on the table. Someone must be out here with her.

Sonya noted how fresh wood had been recently added to the campfire. Jody and whoever accompanied her couldn't be far away. Chances are they were walking by the lake. Sonya could see the little paths leading to the water through trees and foliage, but she rejected the notion of looking for the two on those dark trails.

She skirted the immediate area, stopping by the primitive toilets to call Jody's name. Only silence.

Even if they'd gone off in someone's car, they would, no doubt, return soon. Sonya seated herself rigidly on the bench protected from the rain by a drooping, overhead roof. She sat with her back to the table, eyes locked on the fire. Its flickering spurts un-nerved her. Again, she had an impression of being watched — a sensation growing ominously stronger.

Jolted by a faint sound, she stood up.

Was that the crackle of the fire, or did a footstep fall against dry twigs?

She listened breathlessly, eyes alert. Anger at Jody returned with great intensity.

Jody's out there, watching me! Somewhere in that thick growth of cottonwoods lining the bank. She could sense it. Did Jody intend to remain hidden until Sonya grew tired of waiting and left?

Determined to outwait her cousin, Sonya reclaimed her place on the bench. She judged the passing of time only by her own rapid thoughts. Was it possible that Jody and some unknown person had been working together to get what they could from Uncle Alex?

Sonya heard a distinct crunch of heavy step against dead branch. This time she detected the exact place of the sound. She rose and faced a solitary form moving from out of the trees and advancing toward her.

"The very last person I want to see."

Jody's voice, neither friendly nor un-friendly, addressed her. Jody stepped into the fire's light, and it played uncertainly across long, loose hair, shone across high cheekbones and broad forehead.

"Aren't there any other campers here?"

"On the other side of the lake there's an old couple fishing."

"You shouldn't be staying out here alone," Sonya said, then, glance dropping to the dishes, added, "or are you alone?"

Jody's voice became sarcastic.

"Don't you have business of your own to mind?"

"I've decided to rent a motel room for you for a week or so."

"How nice of you."

Jody turned away from Sonya, bent, and rummaged through a box of clothes, then pulled on a man's shirt over her sleeveless one. "But don't bother. I'm a person who needs fresh air and lake water."

"Aren't you afraid to stay out here?"

"Aren't you afraid to stay with those creeps Alex took up with?"

Jody faced her again as she spoke. Standing defiantly straight, Jody, in the large shirt, looked very thin and very young, as if she needed protection from a world she knew very little about. Only an illusion, Sonya thought. She studied Jody a while before she asked, "Who's here with you?"

"Absolutely no one."

She can lie so easily.

"Then there's no reason why we can't drive into Linnville and rent you a room."

Jody's huge eyes caught the gleam of fire.

"I needed you when I asked you for a loan. I don't now, so why don't you just be on your way?"

"Connie told me you'd stopped by the house. I just wondered why."

"Not to see you. I wanted to talk to Connie."

"What about?"

"That's not your concern."

"I went to a lot of trouble finding you, Jody. We should talk. We need to work together and try to help Uncle Alex."

"That's your job, not mine." The words were sprinkled with bitterness.

"You lied to me about how long you've been in town. Why didn't you see Alex back in December?"

"Because, I'm not you, Sonya. He's never once in his life ever wanted to see me. It's only you he wants to see."

Sonya, smacked by Jody's spitefulness, suddenly believed in her cousin's guilt. Of course she would sneak into Alex's house and steal from him. Sonya pictured Jody peddling Anna's items of treasured memories to street riffraff. The idea filled her with anger and disgust.

"Jody, what on earth made you steal from him?"

"Why don't you get out of here!"

Jody scooped up dishes and tossed them into a pan with such force that Sonya thought they'd break. This accomplished, she whirled back to Sonya. Spite had changed to hatred.

"You don't like me any better than he does."

"There's not much of our family left. We should stick together."

"Why don't you tell that to Alex? You've tried to estrange me, both of you."

"That's not true, and you know it."

"I know a lot of things you don't think I know. Malroy told me the minute I got to town just what Alex had done."

She sucked in her breath.

"Left the Rathmell place — a tidy little fortune — all to you. Butter up Alex, take it all! Your scheming paid off, didn't it?"

Sonya had never even thought about inheriting from Alex. Jody's accusation took her by surprise.

"I didn't even know about the deed myself

until a few days ago. How did Malroy find out?"

"Alex told him, and Malroy let me know about it just to get my goat."

Jody's voice raised.

"How could you do this to Dan? How could you just snatch his inheritance away from him?"

But it wasn't Dan that Jody was concerned about. Jody's concern was for herself. Sonya could hardly believe Jody had counted so heavily on inheriting from Alex. The knowledge made her feel half-sick.

Jody paced away from her. When she turned back, her eyes glowed cat-like across the campfire.

"What a mistake Alex made," she said, her voice high and irrational. "He should have been leery of you all these years, instead of me. You really ended up with it all, didn't you?"

CHAPTER 16

Deep depression hung over Sonya as she arose the next morning. She came down the stairs, intensely aware of the fact that Alex wouldn't be in the kitchen laughing and mixing hotcakes. Her uncle's tragic absence was made worse by thoughts of Alma lingering between life and death at the Linnville Hospital.

After toast and coffee, she went outside. The air was already layered with waves of heat. Sonya recalled the long, hot Kansas days that had made up her childhood, those carefree years revolving around her father, Alex, Anna, and . . . Dan. Her sadness deepened.

Sonya wandered past Alex's work-shed and, shading her eyes against the glare, looked across the field toward Dan's cabin. The wheat, covering the sharp rise of hillside separating them, had almost overnight become tinged with gold.

The moment she'd left the house, Sonya realized she'd been hoping, even half-expecting, to find Dan. She took a few uncertain steps along the rutted road but soon stopped, distracted by the laborious, clanking sound of an engine near the building behind her.

Melvin LaVett, on an ancient green tractor, called to her as he pulled in close to the shed.

"Sonya, I'm spraying the orchard today."

He jumped down agilely, unlocked the door, and returned to the entrance carrying a sprayer and a can of spray which he poured into the tank while he talked.

"Why don't you come with me?"

"I've got some business I must see to."

"This won't delay you long. Some fresh air will do you good."

Sonya drew closer to where he mixed the spray. Just behind him in Alex's work-shed she identified patches of gleaming mahogany. The old windup phonograph, which Anna had on occasion allowed her to play, had once set in the center of the ballroom. Now, amid the clutter, half covered with torn canvas, it seemed pitifully abandoned. She wondered if it still worked and if Alex had set it out here because this is where he spent much of his time and because it reminded him of Anna.

Melvin worked silently. Task soon completed, he locked the shed and climbed back on the tractor seat, extending his hand to her.

It had been so long since she'd seen the orchard. What harm could it do if she went along? On impulse, Sonya accepted his assistance.

Melvin's white-toothed smile made him look young and appealing.

"You can't stand up hanging on to the wheel. Here, sit on my lap."

He drew her to his knee, reached around her, and started the engine again.

Sonya could see over the narrow front of the tractor's two tiny wheels. At any moment she expected the ill-proportioned old relic to topple over.

As they hit a deep rut, she held on to Melvin to keep from falling, and the clumsy, uncertain motions of the tractor forbade her letting go of him. She wanted to talk to him, but the clattering noise prohibited any conversation.

She soon glimpsed Dan's cabin, looking forlorn and alone. She wondered if he would still be asleep. She pictured him, black hair against the white of the pillow, just awakening. She knew he enjoyed living in the center of the farm. From the wide-open windows he could hear the meadow larks, or at night, the yelp of coyotes.

Melvin swung the tractor to the right, and they descended a shadowy, dirt trail infringed upon by weeds and erosion. The path ended in the isolation of the orchard. The motor died with the flick of the key.

Melvin sprang to the ground, and strong, muscular arms lifted her from the tractor. He'd been right. The air, cooler in the draw, refreshed her. He unfastened the tank while Sonya admired his quick, certain movements.

The orchard, a project of John T. Rathmell's, had once been grand and impressive, but now, like the house, it reeked of neglect. The scattering of apple trees, whose blossoms bobbed with intermittent breezes channeled by the slope of hillside, looked wild and unattended.

"I'm spraying for apple maggots. That brownish pulp you see on the fruit is caused by them."

Melvin turned away from her to adjust a hose as he spoke. "I worked in an orchard in California before I came here."

Sonya smiled.

"Most people wouldn't trade California for Kansas."

"Kansas suits me."

He straightened up, his quick smile appearing again. "I've been everywhere, and I think I've finally found a place to settle down. You should see what I'm doing with the old Bailey house. This road, you know, connects with my land."

"Are you buying Bailey's farm?"

"I only rent, but I keep everything in good repair because it's my home."

He set down the sprayer and wiped his hands against tight, faded jeans.

"My next project'll be helping Alex fix up the house."

"It looks as if he intends to sell out."

"I'll have to see the transaction take place before I'll believe it. Alex does plan on moving to Circle Street for a while. Then he'll drift back. This place is his life."

"But . . ."

"It'd be great fun restoring the mansion."

Sonya loved the beautiful old homes from the past. Melvin's same interest served to draw them closer together. He continued to talk as he fiddled with the sprayer.

"The house needs so much work. Just like the orchard."

She watched Melvin for a while in silence, finally asking, "Does Alex hire you to take care of the orchard?"

He laughed.

"If Alex had any cash, he'd put it to better use. I like him, so I help him. Besides, who knows, I may pick enough apples to do some canning."

"Dan and I used to pick fruit here."

At the mention of Dan's name, Melvin's smile vanished.

She pushed the mention of Dan a little further.

"Believe it or not, Alex and he were a good team once. This place looked so much different then."

"Let's not ruin the morning talking about him."

Melvin unloaded the sprayer, absently, as if his mind was no longer on his work. "You wouldn't want to hear my opinion of Dan Rathmell."

With a suddenness that surprised her, Melvin set down the heavy tank. The frown on his face vanished slowly. He reached above him to an overhead branch and snapped off a twig thick with whitish blossoms.

"A pretty girl like you should never see or hear anything that isn't beautiful."

I shouldn't have come with him to this isolated place.

Sonya reluctantly accepted the flowers. As

208

she did, his hand closed over hers, and large blue eyes looked at her entreatingly. She moved back slightly, but his hands slid around her waist and began to draw her forward.

The sound of a motor caused him to drop his arms and step back. A black car, driving much too fast for the state of the road, bounced toward them. The vehicle pulled to a stop so close to Sonya she could have touched the hood. The gleaming metal was as neat and polished as Dan himself looked as he stepped from the car.

Sonya couldn't read any emotion in the opaque eyes surveying her.

"You're wanted back at the house."

"Is there news of Alma or Alex?" she asked anxiously.

"No."

"How did you find me?"

"You weren't exactly hidden. Everyone in Linnville can hear that tractor."

Dan's dark eyes locked a baleful gaze on Melvin, who bent to tighten the hose fitting to the tank. Sonya could see his full lips tensely concealing white teeth. Without the smile, Melvin looked stern and determined. He spoke, sharp, authoritative.

"Let's go back to the house."

"I'm heading there anyway. Sonya can —"

"I brought her here," Melvin interrupted. "I'll take her back."

A sudden breeze ruffled Dan's hair and clothing. His straight posture, the sudden squaring of his shoulders, gave him an air of challenge. Sonya felt threatened by the knowledge that when he was sparring with Melvin, unlike the confrontation she had witnessed between him and Alex, Dan was not going to back down.

To avoid an open clash between them, Sonya walked around Dan's car and opened the door. She cast a half-apologetic glance over her shoulder.

"It's too much trouble for you to drive the tractor across the field. I'll just ride with Dan."

Dan, with the same too-rapid pace, swung the vehicle around and, skillfully missing the ruts, followed the tracks through dirt and grass to the top of the hill.

She was curious.

"Does the sheriff want to talk to me?"

Dan made no reply. They were headed toward the barn. Sonya, dreading the sight of charred wood, the lingering odor of smoke, looked away.

Instead of following the road leading across the field to Alex's house, Dan swung the car off to the right.

"Where are you going?"

Again, purposefully, Dan didn't answer. Sonya felt a flush rise to her face, one caused by her sudden resentment of him rather than by the hot air blowing in from the open windows.

In a few short minutes he pulled the vehicle to a stop at the front door of his cabin.

"You said I was wanted at the house."

"I didn't say which house."

With no other words, Dan left the car and disappeared through the entrance.

Uncertain of what to do, Sonya waited for a long time for him to return. When he didn't, she walked hesitantly to the doorway.

"Dan."

The total silence from inside remained unbroken. She stepped cautiously across the threshold.

"Prepare to defend yourself!" Dan called. He sprang forward, lifted her off her feet, and swung her around the center of the room, laughing.

Back on solid ground, Sonya felt his lips claim hers. During the long, breathless kiss, able to forget everything else, she clung to him.

Finally, she attempted to draw away.

"Why did you bring me here?"

Dan stepped back, dark eyebrows raised humorously.

"My dear, your innocence charms me."

Familiar with his teasing, Sonya tried not to return his smile.

Dan gazed at her, his black eyes alight. After a while, in the same joking voice, he spoke.

"Don't you think I get jealous?"

"Jealous?" she repeated.

"We both know I'm in love with you. And what do you do? The very first chance you get, you run off and kiss a stranger."

She bridled at the suggestion.

"I wasn't kissing anyone."

"But could I depend on that?" A mischievous sparkle lit his dark eyes. "I don't think so. So, you see, I had to save you. Just like the knights of old."

"I must have overlooked the danger." Her reply was layered with sarcasm, but she was amused despite herself.

"Women usually do."

"A knight chauvinist," she accused, smiling, enjoying, as always, their easy banter.

Embarrassed by the way he remained, quietly watching, she tried to explain.

"I just wanted to see the orchard again. I can't just ignore Melvin, he is Alex's good friend. I appreciate all that he's done and is still doing. He seems very ambitious."

"So were Caesar's assassins."

She grinned.

"But would they have gotten up so early in the morning to spray the orchard?"

"If you were going along, I'd say 'yes'."

Dan continued to study her in the same solemn manner, then posed her a question.

"Do I detect in your words some comparison between LaVett and me? Are you thinking he's the only one willing to help Alex?"

"After the way Uncle Alex treated you, why would you want to help him?"

He did not reply at once.

"Because what happened between us isn't entirely his fault."

Dan looked away as if he had deep regrets.

"I was so grieved over Mother's death, I didn't even think of him. Now that I have, I realize what a very hard time he had."

Feeling relieved by Dan's confiding this to her, Sonya began to relax, and, for the first time, she looked around the neat study. Low shelves, filled with law books, no doubt taken from his father's office, lined the walls. She wandered toward the desk where an open book lay beside a computer.

Dan followed her. He reached around her and opened the top drawer.

"I told you I'd give you these," he said,

handing her a stack of pictures. "The Rath-mell place in better days."

Dan remembered what she'd told him about the series of articles she was doing on the old, Midwest mansions. How thoughtful of him to help her with her work. Sonya shuffled through the photographs. She soon discovered one that would be certain to enhance her article, one in which Rathmell Place glowed with fresh paint and immaculate care.

She sorted through the others, close-ups, showing details of each room, taken when they'd been furnished, with Anna Rathmell's exquisite taste.

"Thank you, Dan. These are just what I need. They'll complete my first submission."

"I like that one of the ballroom best."

Memories assailed her as she sorted the photograph he'd mentioned out from the others — childhood memories of hiding from Dan and Jody in the cabinet beneath the stairway or behind the flowing velvet drapes.

Dan was smiling.

"Remember when I dressed up in Alex's army uniform and asked you to dance with me?"

His hand brushed hers as he tilted the picture toward her.

"If I recall correctly, you said you'd rather wind the phonograph. I hope you don't still feel that way."

Sonya smiled too.

"The old phonograph probably won't wind any longer."

"On the contrary, it runs like brand new. Alex put it out in his shed because he still likes to play it."

Sonya thought again of Jody, Dan, and her as children. A question emerged.

"Do you know Jody's been in town since before Christmas?"

At the mention of Jody, Dan became suddenly serious.

"What would Jody be doing in Linnville that long?" he asked, his deep voice reflecting the tone of the lawyer he would someday become. "Why would she stay in town and not contact Alex?"

Sonya spoke again, her voice edged with disconcertment.

"There's so many questions that need answers."

"I have some questions, too," Dan said, "and most of them concern Melvin LaVett."

Sonya put down the picture.

"As you know, Alex doesn't trust everyone, but he seems to like and depend on Melvin. Has Melvin been renting from Mr.

Bailey long?"

"A little over a year," Dan replied. "When he first came to town, Alex met him at Malroy's, and they struck up a friendship. Alex was probably responsible for his renting the Bailey farm."

He paused, frowning. "Is there any chance Jody might have known him when she lived in California?"

Sonya shook her head.

"I'm the one who introduced them. If Jody had met him before, then she's become a very good actress."

"Which is possible if she sees enough profit."

Dan studied her again.

"Before you fall too deeply in love, let me try to see what I can find out about LaVett."

His remark sparked resentment.

"You've no reason to be concerned about that!"

"Don't I?" Dan raised a dark eyebrow. "Do you know what Malroy told me yesterday? He said LaVett made the remark that you are the girl he intends to marry!"

He paused, regarding her carefully as if he were trying to read her thoughts. "Instant love, like instant mashed potatoes."

He continued watching for a reaction.

Sonya didn't want to discuss the rivalry

he felt concerning Melvin, and started toward the door.

Dan's deep voice drifted after her.

"I'm the one you ought to marry."

Feeling a strange shortness of breath, she faced him again. Almost against her will, she gazed into the depths of his eyes, aware of his broad shoulders, of his black hair left tousled by the wind. He stepped closer to her, and once more she was enfolded in his arms

"I love you so much, Sonya," he said huskily. "I've always loved you."

His lips against hers left her even more breathless. She wanted with all her heart to answer, *I love you, too.*

But she didn't.

"Am I wrong?" he asked. "Believing we feel the same way about each other?"

"This isn't the right time, Dan."

"I know I haven't much to offer you now. I wanted to wait until I'd finished law school. But . . . waiting — it'll mean that you'll leave here again."

"I just can't discuss this. Not right now."

"For your own good I should be wishing you'd go back to Boston."

"The police won't let me leave town."

"You could stay in a motel, then. After what happened to Alma, you need to think

217

of protecting yourself."

"I wouldn't be any safer in Linnville than I am here. This could end any time, Dan. Alma could come out of the coma and identify the person who tried to kill her."

"Whoever's behind this isn't afraid of Alma. She'll be too scared — for herself or for Connie — to point her finger at anyone. Alex and you are the ones at risk."

"I've tried very hard to locate Uncle Alex. I don't even know if —"

"Don't worry about Alex," Dan interrupted. "He can take care of himself. It's you I'm worried about." His voice became terse and harsh. "You don't seem to realize the danger you're in. Everyone knows you're digging into things you should be leaving alone."

Dan said no more until they were in the car. "Sonya," he said with great feeling, "I want you to marry me. Right away."

CHAPTER 17

Why has Dan asked me to marry him now, with Uncle Alex gone, with Alma dying, with the sheriff on the verge of arresting me?

Sonya shrank against the car door, her gaze fixed on the trail ahead, on the roof of the Rathmell mansion just coming into view over the rise of the hill.

Sunlight glinted against badly deteriorated boards and into unshielded windows as Dan pulled up close to the porch. The old house — so familiar to her, and her childhood companion, Dan, seemed suddenly grim and hostile.

He turned to her, an arm draped over the steering wheel. "Please listen to me, Sonya. I can't make it any clearer. You can't afford to trust anyone, and that warning includes Alex."

Sonya, relieved she didn't have to face Emil and Connie, who must have left for the hospital, entered the silent front room. She sank down on the recliner near the door and tried to sort out her reeling thoughts, to decide what to do next. There she remained for a very long time, totally lost in a maze of unanswered questions.

The shrill ringing of the phone startled her. She waited for a moment, then cautiously lifted the receiver.

"Brighton's residence."

Sonya strained to make out the almost whispered words.

"Is Sonya there?"

"This is Sonya. Who am I talking to?"

"I have something important to tell you."

The voice, so low in volume, spoke without emotion, like some impersonal recording.

Her heart began to pound.

"Alex?"

Even though she spoke his name, Sonya sensed the speaker wasn't her uncle. Alex couldn't disguise the crusty, abrupt way he spoke from her.

"Be at the Talbert mansion at one-o'clock. Make sure you're alone. Bring three hundred dollars in cash."

Cash. Why does that make me think of Jody?

"Who is this?" Gripped by a slight panic,

she waited tensely for an answer. Despite the total silence, someone remained on the line.

"Are you calling for Jody?"

A harsh click sounded, followed by a steady buzzing.

Could the message possibly be from Uncle Alex?

Feeling slightly dizzy, Sonya rose. She paced around the room, then on impulse returned to the phone and called Bill Cole.

A terse, 'Hello' — Bill must've been right beside the phone — followed the first ring.

"This is Sonya Brighton. We were cut off."

Sonya pictured Bill as he'd looked at his home the night she'd searched for Alex. His stern, military composure was revealed by the slow, clear pace of his words.

"You must be mistaken."

"Please be truthful. I'm sure you've been in contact with my uncle. I simply must know if you were the one who called me a minute ago."

A heavy quietness lingered between them.

"Is he hiding because he knows who set the warehouse fire? You've heard about Alma Steelman. We're dealing with a very desperate person. I must get some answers."

"I'm not the one to give them to you."

With that brief sentence, with not even an

added 'Goodbye', Bill Cole hung up. His cold evasiveness led Sonya to believe that Alex had asked him to make the call. The thought brought with it relief.

It means Uncle Alex is safe.

Sonya checked her watch — almost eleven. She didn't have much time. She'd need to go into Linnville before starting off for Talbert.

The momentary joy she felt soon became tinged with fear. If the message had been from Alex, how was she going to avoid leading someone to him? If the speaker hadn't been calling for her uncle, then this could be some kind of setup, not for Alex, but for her.

Sonya tried to calm her runaway thoughts with reason. If someone meant to harm her, he certainly wouldn't choose a populated place like the Talbert Mansion. In any event, she had only two choices. She must either ignore the call or head to Talbert.

In Sonya's heart, however sinister the whispered words of a clandestine meeting sounded, she knew she was going to keep the appointment.

Dark clouds, able to appear so quickly and unexpectedly in a Kansas sky, had formed overhead.

Sonya stopped at the Linnville Bank and cashed three hundred dollars worth of her traveler's checks. She decided against taking the highway but opted for the back road that would wind through small farming communities before reaching the small city of Talbert.

This route led her past the Baxter County Lake where Jody was staying.

Sonya kept glancing in the rearview mirror. She watched headlights glisten on the wet pavement and found herself intentionally slowing down. Cars, hurling sprays of water against her windshield, breezed past, and each time they disappeared into the distance ahead of her, she felt profound relief.

After she'd passed the turnoff to the lake, there was no other traffic. Aloneness made the long, flat horizon seem less threatening, and she began to breathe much easier.

The rain that had been lashing across her car had let up a little, but the sky had grown continually darker. Sonya could barely make out the misty outline of the overpass just ahead, but she could read the sign, 'Talbert, 10 miles', and see the black arrow directing motorists to the main highway.

Sonya somehow felt more secure on the old road.

As she approached the overpass, she was startled by an unidentifiable noise from directly above her. An explosive clack, like the backfiring of a car, sounded again, loud this time and very close.

To her dismay she saw no vehicle on the road above her. It took her only moments to realize what she was hearing wasn't a car — it was the blasting of a firearm.

Her heart plummeted. A sniper lay hidden just above her. At this very moment, the barrel of a gun was aimed at her. Impulsively she swerved her car off to the right. Just as she did, another shot sounded. Maybe if she hadn't reacted so quickly, the bullet would have pierced the windshield and struck her.

Sonya jammed down on the gas pedal and plunged straight ahead. She could hear the whiz of a bullet right before she entered the underpass. Then everything fell momentarily silent, even from the pelting rain.

Sonya pressed forward with reckless speed. She didn't dare to even glance behind her. Her only chance lay in beating whoever was shooting at her to Talbert.

The wheels of her car slid on the wet pavement as she slowed for a fast-approaching curve.

It would be wise to change her course.

She tried to remember the layout of the country roads.

After going a mile or so, she swung off to the right and cut across to a graveled section — a road which she believed would eventually connect with the main highway.

She followed a long, meandering course that at last reached the interstate. She felt a gleam of hope when she finally spotted Talbert in the distance, a spattering of lights through the rain. Alertly, she took note of the buildings; 'Ace Self Storage', 'Wagon's West Café', numerous fast food stores typical of a middle-sized, Kansas town.

She circled the block and pulled the car to a stop in front of the police station.

Sonya hurried inside and said to the young uniformed man behind the desk, "I want to report a shooting on the old Linnville road."

With a good deal of alarm, as if such incidents were not common to their little community, he radioed a police car. Afterwards he asked her endless questions, which he recorded on a form that he eventually asked her to sign.

When the policeman finally allowed her to leave, Sonya took a back exit. If whoever had shot at her had continued on to Talbert, chances were he'd be watching her car.

She would leave it parked out front and walk the several blocks to the Talbert Mansion.

A whirlwind of questions bombarded Sonya as she took a careful, circuitous route to her destination.

Was the person who talked to me on the phone the same person who shot at me? Or was it someone who'd been listening to my conversation with Bill Cole and wants to prevent me meeting with Uncle Alex?

The only other possibility would be that the would-be killer had been watching her for some time, that he had followed her from Linnville. He could have been inside one of the vehicles that had swerved around her. He could have sped on ahead and waited for her at the overpass.

Sonya ducked into an alley, where she waited, intently watching. Satisfied no one was trailing her, she headed on again.

Once the mansion came into view, Sonya stopped and drew in her breath. After her bare escape with death, she'd have to be out of her mind to be keeping this appointment.

Chapter 18

In front of the Talbert Mansion, protected from the rain by an overhead balcony, sightseers with hooded raincoats and umbrellas clustered. Sonya hurried across the street to join them, pausing once to look behind her, across the square where the twin spires of a Catholic church loomed, crosses lost in an eerie mist.

She searched through the scattering of people for a glimpse of Alex's craggy face or rigid form. She pressed her shoulder-strap purse close to her side and stopped short before she reached the huge porch. Alex, if the message she had received had been from him, had asked for only three-hundred dollars. She now questioned if the amount she'd cashed from her travelers' checks would be sufficient. But why did she worry about that now? The only concern of any importance was whether or not Alex was going to show up.

She waited impatiently, easing around the milling crowd of sixteen or eighteen, to see if he had somehow managed to remain unnoticed among them. Satisfied that he hadn't, she found herself once again standing away from the entrance.

Reluctantly, Sonya removed the camera from her purse. She might just as well make use of the waiting, take pictures for the article she must soon send to Dexter Publications. However, her heart wasn't in the diversion.

Fine rain sprayed against her face as she looked up at the mansion. Despite her increasing worry, a little of the old awe splendid buildings always caused in her surfaced. From the ingress, a single high tower rose in splendid, high Victorian style. Directly overhead, a balcony stretched along the vast right side of the house and across the porch, its thick wall lined with ornate marble pots and vases, some of immense size. Various shapes and weights were balanced to obtain a symmetry pleasing to the eye.

The left wing of the house, having no balcony, was decorated by huge bay windows. The entire effect was highly picturesque, reminding her of architect Alexander Davis and the fashion popular just after the

Civil War. The style, however, seemed to be mixed, a little of the Gothic revival showing in the delicate elegance of detail, sloping eves trimmed with pendants. Overdone, she thought, comparing it with the massive solidness of the Rathmell Place.

Her gaze returned to a huge, white vase directly in line with the sidewalk. She thought of old movies where a killer lurked overhead, waiting for the moment he could hurl some heavy object down upon an unsuspecting victim. The thought caused a weakness in her legs.

Why has Alex, if it is Alex, suggested we meet here?

Inside, the old house would be laced with passageways. Walls would have hidden recesses, dark alcoves, perfect for concealing some awaiting attacker.

The guide, a frail man with white hair and skin, stood in the center of the porch area, as if waiting for her to step forward and join the others. As she did, he began speaking in a voice that matched his gentlemanly air.

"Russell Talbert was a lover of marble. The marble you see," he indicated the gigantic flower vase just above them, "was carefully selected during Mr. Talbert's many journeys around the world. That very white, pure marble was obtained directly from Italy."

His speech continued, but for her, the sound of his voice receded. She checked her watch — already one-fifteen. Uncle Alex should have shown up by now.

Sonya, the last to enter the mansion, looked back once again toward the rainy street. Inside, a stairway of gleaming black marble, the first resting place for the eye upon entering, wound upward. She bought a ticket from the white-haired lady at the desk and listened to the guide. With voice slow and soothing, he spoke of the heavy, brass-plated French doors leading off the front room into the dining area. They were open and through the doorway Sonya could see the west entrance to the house and a hallway, where shielded doorways were hung with multicolored beads.

As the tour wore on, Sonya automatically wrote into her note pad facts she wouldn't be able to remember, snapped her pictures, and lost hope of Alex's ever meeting her.

She followed the long line of tourists upstairs. At the top of the stairway, a long corridor, walls hung with family portraits, made sharp right angles in both directions. She lingered near the top of the steps, then began to trail after the last of the group.

"Sonya."

The voice came from the unoccupied corridor to her west. She whirled back, but the immediate area was empty. The hushed voice spoke her name again. Sonya hurried around the corner and came face to face with Uncle Alex.

Relief flooded through her. She'd never been so glad to see anyone.

Alex — he must have stepped back after calling to her — stood stiffly in the middle of the hallway. Tears blurred her vision as she spoke.

"I'm so glad to see you."

"Same here."

He drew slowly forward. She'd somehow expected the absence to have changed him, that he would no longer be casually calm, possessed of that droll humor characterizing him. He stood before her, safe. The familiar sight of his lined face, which, even when serious, bore the indelible markings of a smile, made her reach out and embrace him. She said apprehensively, "You took a chance calling like that. And why did you choose the Talbert Mansion of all places?"

"Bill did the calling. This is all I could manage."

"I've been worried sick. Why did you disappear like that?"

Alex's gaze settled on her for a few seconds before he answered in his curt way.

"I've gotten used to being alive."

Sonya was tempted to tell him about her own experience but decided against it. She didn't want him worrying about her. He must concentrate on protecting himself.

"If your life's in danger, our meeting here is foolhardy."

Once again he cut her short.

"I've got to do what I've got to do. Did you bring the money?"

"I hope this is enough."

Alex took the bills from her and counted them.

"Enough for now."

"Have you heard about Alma?"

He avoided looking at Sonya as he asked, "What are her chances of coming out of the coma?"

"Not good."

Not wanting to tell Alex all the details of the fire, how she had placed herself at great risk, she hurried on, "Did you know Jody's in town?"

"Don't add to my torment," he said. His frosty eyes held to the guide, who had just stepped into their line of vision and stopped to address the crowd.

Sonya wanted him to know.

"I found out that Jody was in Linnville before Christmas, at the time you were robbed."

Retaining the same expression, Alex's gaze shifted to her. She'd expected some angry reaction from her announcement and waited for him to speak, but when he did, his words didn't concern Jody.

"That night when we got back from the fire, I went out to the work-shed. That's where I go when I can't sleep. And . . ."

He drawled, as if they had endless time available for their discussion, "these days that's becoming more and more often. I'd started to wind up the old phonograph, another mental health aid, when someone hidden behind those stacks of furniture knocked me over and ran out."

"Could you identify him?"

"No, he came at me from behind. I think I know who it was."

Even though he hadn't named Dan, the accusation present in his voice caused a chill to run through her.

He still watched the guide as he continued.

"Right away I began to figure some things out."

"What?"

Alex paused.

"Someone was inside the shed that night planning to meet his coconspirator — the one he had hired for a small sum to do his dirty work, to burn the warehouse and frame me for arson. He was waiting there to pay off his hired hand when I walked in."

"Could Emil have been the one who attacked you?"

Mingled voices of the crowd as they proceeded into the corridor prevented further talk. Automatically, almost guiltily, Sonya reached for her camera and snapped several pictures.

The guide gave her a faint smile. The brilliant flash of light magnified his paleness, made him seem a ghost lingering in the place generation after generation.

"These statues make lovely photographs," he remarked.

Lagging behind the others, she and Alex moved forward with the last of the group.

"That night when I made it back inside the house, I got my gun and called Bill to pick me up. I'm convinced that if I'd decided to stay in that house, I'd be dead now."

Sonya regarded him closely. Her uncle continued to watch the guide, not even glancing toward her. Her heart sank. What if Alex had been waiting for the man he had himself hired to set the fire? Angry over the bungled job, he might have refused to make final payment. Somehow he could have gotten away from his enraged partner in crime and thought it best to go into hiding.

No! Alex would never be involved in such dealings.

"We'd better go right now and talk to the sheriff," she advised him. "I think he'll believe us. Let's let him do the investigating."

"Davis?" Alex asked with disbelief. "You are hoping for a miracle, aren't you? If I want the truth, I'm going to have to find it out for myself. I've got Bill working on something right now that might link the arsonist with the fire."

Alex turned to face her. She stared at him.

"You think Dan's guilty, don't you?"

"It sure looks that way. But it doesn't make any difference what anyone thinks, only what can be proven. The only thing I know for sure is that someone removed the furs before the warehouse burned."

Alex's statement confirmed her suspicions — the expensive furs had been removed before the fire. Even at a portion of their value, the furs would net many thousands of dollars, a grand sum for someone like Jody or Emil. But if what Alex believed were true, finding the stolen goods or tracing what had become of them would be virtually impossible. They could have been fenced at the same time they had been removed.

Alex eyed a beautiful figurine moodily.

"I keep thinking about the day Dan, Melvin, and I went to Kansas City to look at that garage Melvin wanted to rent for a repair shop."

"Dan was with you?"

When Dan and Sonya had looked for the building the day he'd accompanied her to Kansas City, Sonya had thought it unusual that he'd been able to find the exact location so easily. Now she wondered why Dan hadn't told her he'd been there before.

"Who owns the garage?" she asked.

"An old widow named Mona Troy. She doesn't know the first thing about business and is often out of the state. Bill's been trying to reach her but hasn't had any luck. In the mean time, he's been checking out the storage rental places in the hopes of running across a familiar name."

The guide reappeared, his leading the group out of the first bedroom and back into the hallway, silencing Alex.

The man droned on as he swept past.

"In the cases along the west wall of Mrs. Talbert's bedroom, you will see her doll collection. The largest one, in the center of the display, belonged to Mrs. Talbert's mother, and was brought here from Lund, Sweden."

"You mustn't go on with this search alone. You're going to . . ."

Sonya's whispered words faded. Then, knowing she must appeal to something besides his own safety, she continued.

"You're going to place Bill in danger, too."

"Bill and I have gone through minefields together."

She tried to impress him with the danger they were facing.

"Someone could have followed me here. They could be waiting outside now so they can find out where you're staying. Alex, you must give up this investigation. You'll be killed."

Sonya must have spoken the last words too loudly. The couple just ahead of them turned to stare, first at her then at Uncle Alex. Sonya lowered her voice.

"Who would have keys to the warehouse besides you, Bill, and me?"

He answered immediately.

"Dan. Right after he robbed me, I missed my spare set of keys."

Sonya waited for the guide to usher the crowd into the far bedroom before she spoke again.

"If I find out anything, I'll need to contact

you. Where are you staying?"

He side-stepped the question.

"If I had once thought you were in danger, I never would have left the house. Even now, I'm convinced you're safe only if you stay completely out of this. That's exactly what I want you to do. Come on. Let's go."

On the bottom floor, the white-haired lady, from whom Sonya had purchased her ticket, still sat by the door.

"I hope you enjoyed your tour," she said pleasantly.

"We did," Alex answered as he passed her. Without looking back, he moved in his slow, stiff way across the porch.

Sonya froze in fear. She had images of Alex, fallen and bloody, and of a broken marble vase, flowers uprooted, dirt strewn across the sidewalk. She caught up with him just before he stepped out on to the sidewalk.

She went around him and looked up. No movement from above caught her eye. The white marble basin, like some giant still-life painting blending into the foggy air, remained securely on the ledge.

Her fingers tightened fearfully on Alex's arm as they walked away from the house.

"I'm afraid," she said.

"You're my niece," he answered. "You can

take care of yourself."

She glanced furtively over her shoulder, then back at him.

"I'm afraid for you."

"Don't be."

An expression of affection caused deep creases to form around his eyes. "I'm going to leave now. You just keep out of this, and everything will turn out all right. I'll be in touch."

Sonya watched him walk through the mist toward the road. At the same time a battered, old truck pulled up, and Alex got inside.

At the curb, Sonya stood in the rain looking up and down the quiet street. No traffic passed. She allowed herself to take a deep breath, of air scented with damp earth. For now, at least, Uncle Alex was alive and well. And so was she.

Temporarily.

CHAPTER 19

Connie, with Emil looming in the shadowy background just behind her, met Sonya at the door.

"I've got great news," Connie said. "Alma spoke to us this afternoon. She's going to be all right."

Sonya felt a rush of great relief. "I'm so glad to hear that."

They both looked at her as if not quite sure her joyous reaction was genuine.

"Did Alma talk to the sheriff?" Sonya asked. "Was she able to make any statement?"

"Alma didn't see anything," Emil said flatly.

"How could she? The poor girl was struck from behind."

After a long pause, with voice edged with indignation, Connie went on.

"Whoever hit her started that fire and left her there to die. If it wasn't for you, Sonya,

Alma would be dead. That's just what I told the sheriff."

Emil spoke again, his voice flat and cold.

"The sheriff's been looking for you all afternoon."

"We didn't know where you were, Sonya. Then Henry got this call from the Talbert Police Department."

Sonya glanced from Connie to Emil. Emil did not look at her directly, yet he was watching in his tense, sly way, as if she were some opponent in the ring.

She explained.

"Someone shot at me this afternoon. From the Linnville-Talbert overpass."

"That's what Henry told us. He went right out there, but he couldn't find any empty shells or anything."

Connie paused, then stared boldly at her.

"Sonya, I'm going to tell you the truth. Henry believes you just made the story up."

"Is that what he told you?"

"He didn't have to," Connie replied. She stopped and looked back at Emil, as if she expected him to pick up the story from there.

"The sheriff's going to bring arson charges against you," Emil said shortly. "Against you and Alex."

Even though his expression didn't change,

Sonya couldn't fail to note the glint of satisfaction that had come into his eyes.

Feeling the impact of this jarring news, she moved quickly toward the stairway.

Connie's words trailed after her.

"I just don't think you had anything to do with setting that fire, Sonya."

Connie hesitated, then, "I'm not so sure about Alex, but for you, it just doesn't seem right. And that's just what I said to Henry Davis."

A few hours later, unable to sleep, Sonya came back downstairs. Neither Connie or Emil remained in the front room. She wandered outside toward Alex's work-shed.

The hasp clung loosely to the deteriorated wood of the door. After several attempts she was able to free the padlock from the frame.

Sonya switched on the dim overhead light and thought of Uncle Alex's being out here the night of the fire. She could picture him turning to the old windup phonograph, selecting one of the thick, worn records, winding the machine at the same slow pace — all while someone watched. Sonya imagined a lurking figure in the shadows, a criminal who couldn't afford to be discovered here by Alex, hiding, waiting for a chance to escape, but knowing he'd soon be discovered.

The shadeless bulb dimly lit the dark corners where furniture was randomly stacked — in one an empty wardrobe, huge enough to conceal a man, one as large as Emil Steelman.

But what had this hidden figure been doing in the shed that night? Just as Alex had said, he must have been waiting to meet his co-conspirator, no doubt the person he'd hired to remove the furs and burn the warehouse. They'd planned to meet here after the fire for the payoff.

Alex had told her that he, unaware someone else was in the shed with him, had started to play the phonograph that night. Sonya approached the old Victrola and removed the torn canvas cover. The brownish-red wood, although marred, still possessed that highly-polished look. She thought of how precious the machine had always been to her, of her great happiness, when under Anna's watchful supervision, she had been allowed to play it.

Sonya, longing for the old days, smoothed her hand over the worn case. She opened the lid and read the label on the battered Victor record inside. 'The Mother's Prayer, Alma Gluck'. She gave the old crank several twists. The turntable merely scraped tiredly and didn't revolve at all. Both Alex and Dan had spoken of the phonograph as still in working condition, unless it had very recently been damaged.

She wound the crank again, then lifted the record and examined the turntable. She rotated it with her fingers and found she could barely force it to turn. Sonya removed the turntable, which came off easily in her hand. Underneath it, she found an envelope.

No wonder it wouldn't spin!

She lifted the business-sized envelope, thick and bulky — full, no doubt, of business papers Alex hadn't wanted anyone to find.

Sonya tore open the seal. She drew in her breath sharply as she found a thick bundle of crisp, one-hundred-dollar bills. Hands trembling, she attempted to count them, but too anxious to complete the job, she simply estimated several thousand dollars.

The hired arsonist hadn't received his final payment. He'd searched the mansion looking for the money his partner had hidden from him. Definitely the partner, whose idea this had been, had refused to make payment because of the bungled job. But if the two of them were at odds, then what had become of the furs?

Sonya had no sooner posed the question

than she spotted a key tucked into the corner of the envelope. She held it up to the light to examine — it was a common key to an old lock, probably to the building where the hired criminal had stored the furs he'd removed before burning the Brighton Warehouse.

Because of finding Anna's ring in Dan's cabin, Alex believed Dan must be behind these robberies, too. But regardless of who'd plotted the warehouse fire, Alex knew he was in grave danger. The attack on Alma certainly proved that to be true — the thief had no qualms about killing. He wouldn't think twice about murdering Alex, who he'd already identified as his opponent.

Sonya's head began to swim.

What will I do now?

Would turning the money and the key over to the sheriff help Alex's position, or would Henry Davis just assume that Alex had been waiting in the shed to talk to the person he himself had hired? And the sheriff was going to maintain she'd been Alex's partner all along.

Sonya's stiff fingers returned the money to the envelope and replaced it beneath the turntable. It had worked as a hiding place up to now; she could think of no better place to conceal it. The key she tucked into her pocket.

Sonya hurried inside just as Alex must have done the night of the fire. She closed the door to his study and sank down at his desk. Today's *Linnville Journal* lay spread in front of her. Her eyes skimmed the dark headlines. The warehouse was still making the feature story. 'Suspicious Fire Under Investigation'. She drew the paper closer and read, *'An investigator from the State Fire Marshall's office is assisting local arson investigators sift through the blackened debris of the Brighton warehouse.'*

Sonya took the key from her pocket and studied it. Suddenly the garage Alex had been thinking of renting in Kansas City, the one Dan had taken her to see, sprang to mind. Impulsively she reached for the phone and asked information for Kansas City, Missouri. Obtaining Mona Troy's number, she dialed it and was surprised when the voice of an elderly woman answered.

"Hello. This is Mona Troy."

"Hello, I'm . . . Melanie Wittersen. I'm sorry to be calling so late, but I've been trying to reach you for some time," Sonya said. "I'm very interested in renting the garage you own on Market Street."

"Dear, it's already occupied."

"Oh. How long has it been rented?"

"For two months. But I really don't think they plan to open the station again."

"Then maybe I could buy out the lease," Sonya suggested.

"Oh, there's no lease. I've just been renting it from month to month."

"Would you mind telling me whom I could contact about it?"

"You know, it's funny, I've never met the couple who rented the building. At first, this woman called and said the place is just what they wanted. Then I got a cashier's check and a message to leave the key in the mailbox at the garage."

"Who was the check from?" Sonya asked anxiously.

"A man from Linnville," the woman answered promptly. "A Dan Rathmell."

Chapter 20

Sonya thanked the woman and replaced the phone, pain like a dagger of ice striking her heart.

Alex had been right about him all along. An image of Dan loomed in her mind, a man she'd loved and trusted.

He's guilty!

What else could she believe now? It had been Dan who'd stolen from her uncle right after Anna's funeral and Alex's stroke. Stealing the furs was just a continuation of what he'd started the moment his mother had died and he'd been disinherited.

Tears brimmed in her eyes. Dan had not only robbed and deceived Uncle Alex, but he'd deceived her, too. His sudden proposal — the rush to marry her — had been only because he'd found out about Alex's deeding the Rathmell Place to her. He was ruthlessly pursuing his determination to keep the mansion for himself. Everything for himself. How little that sounded like the boy she'd met so long ago, how unlike the man she'd grown to love.

Dan had been waiting in the shed the night of the fire to meet and pay off the arsonist he'd hired. Furious because the job had been completed in such an amateurish fashion, Dan had refused to make the final payment, had probably even excluded his partner from his share of the sale of the furs that were already in Dan's possession. Certain of an investigation, Dan then attempted to frame Alex by placing the gas cans in his car.

Or maybe . . . maybe Dan waiting there to be paid off himself?

Alarmed when Alex walked in instead of the man who'd hired him, Dan had simply struck out at him and run away.

Sonya's whirlwind thoughts left her sick and shaken. A woman had called to rent the building in Kansas City. Dan and Jody could have met in Linnville before Christmas and plotted these thefts together. Jody with her daring nature would think it a small task to remove the furs and burn the warehouse.

Unloosed, Sonya's thoughts began to race. The only reason Dan had gone with her to Kansas City was to prevent her from becoming suspicious of Mona Troy's old garage. She could never believe Dan had been trying to kill her, though. He must have shot at her from the overpass just to frighten her into abandoning her investigation.

It had been Dan or his accomplice who'd been searching Alex's house for the remainder of the payoff money, money actually hidden in the phonograph. The attack on Alma made sense, too, if she'd overheard the two guilty parties talking and had threatened to tell the sheriff.

Sonya struggled for calmness and control. She was only assuming the furs were stored in the Kansas City garage. Before her accusations went any further, she must go there and find out if her suspicions were even valid. She went in search of her car keys and jacket.

Rain had started again as she headed toward Kansas City, first as a light drizzle. Headlights from passing traffic reflected on the damp, glistening highway. Very soon her vision became obscured by a downpour, and she found herself leaning tensely forward in the seat, agitated by the steady droning back-and-forth movements of the windshield wipers.

Headlights moved out from behind and passed, speeding onward; none of them remaining long. No car followed as she turned to the side street that she and Dan had taken the day they'd looked at the garage. She soon lost her course but, finally after a long search, intercepted Market Street, turning west. The rundown buildings, isolated by storm and darkness, began to look familiar. She parked under the awning in front of the garage, where water dripped through and made puddles on the concrete drive.

Sonya hadn't thought to bring her raincoat. The dash to the doorway and the fumbling with the key left her wet and shivering. The lock, old and rusty, turned after several tries.

Inside, she was greeted by the strong smell of grease. Coldness and dampness had settled over the area. Sonya stood in the darkness for a moment, aware of the pounding of rain against the metal roof. Seeking for a light switch, she ran her hand along the wall. At last, eyes growing accustomed to the darkness, she noticed an old-style light fixture dangling from a long cord, operated by a pull chain. She was relieved to find that it worked.

Dim light illuminated cartons of various shapes and sizes. Some of the rows along the back wall loomed in stacks almost reaching the ceiling. Other boxes set solitarily around her feet.

Reluctantly, knowing what she'd find inside, Sonya knelt by the nearest one and begin to unseal the packing tape that bound it. Her throat felt constricted, as it had at funerals when she'd tried her best to keep from crying.

Even though Sonya was prepared for what she would see, she nevertheless felt jolted by the glimmer of light upon silver fur. She lifted the expensive jacket, then, standing, let it fall back across the open box.

She scanned the mass of cartons again. She remembered the Brighton Warehouse inventory — mink, unborn calf, fox, ermine — a fortune once the right buyer was contacted. Dan had robbed the furs from the warehouse, just as he had the goods from the Brighton household. Now these furs belonged to him as if they hadn't belonged to Alex and her — all money obtained from them profit, free and clear.

Tears filled her eyes at the thought of Dan. He hadn't done this for money. This was his way of getting revenge on Uncle Alex for the love and trust Anna had placed in him.

Dan had equated inheriting the house and its contents with his mother's love, assuming that in her final act, she'd chosen between them and set Alex above him.

Sonya could even understand the jealousy and hurt Dan had felt over being disinherited, but she couldn't begin to sympathize with what Dan had done to Alma.

Alma, who, always around, must have overheard a conversation between Dan and whoever was working with him.

Tears flowed freely, and Sonya wiped at them as she approached a second box. Absorbed, struggling somewhat angrily with the tape, Sonya was startled by the rapid, scraping sound of the door behind her being pushed open. She reacted quickly, reaching out for the light chain and plunging the garage into darkness.

The engulfing blackness started a fearful pounding in her temples. She edged backward, shrinking against the high cartons lining the wall. The door, wide open, caught by a gust of wind, creaked plaintively back and forth, then slammed shut with a resounding thud.

She remained motionless.

"Sonya!"

She recognized Dan's deep voice at once, calling out to her. She didn't answer. Didn't move.

Her first thought was to make a dash to

the entrance. But, behind the swinging illumination of a flashlight she could now make out Dan's form standing squarely in the center of the room, able to block any attempt at escape.

She held her breath. Dan spotted the light directly above him and yanked the chain. The quick motion caused the overhead bulb to sway back and forth. His face, first clarified, then shadowed, made him look frightening, like some evil stranger.

Dan's dark hair, wet from the rain, and his eyes, black and intent, glistened with the changing light. Total emptiness replaced the fear she had a moment ago felt.

"I guess I was right in following you tonight," he said. His gaze fastened on her steadily, as if he were trying to determine just how much she knew — then dropped to the box she'd just opened.

"I see you've found the furs."

Sonya couldn't bring herself to respond. The silence lingering between them filled with memories. His blue shirt clung to his broad chest, soaking wet. She thought of the pair of them swimming in the pond, of his kiss.

No matter what he was capable of doing to someone else, he surely didn't intend to harm her.

Dan's straightness, his intent solemnness, caused her to remember how he had looked as a boy, his slender frame lost in Alex's army uniform.

"You can't just say 'no'. You've got to dance with me," he'd informed her. "I'm a general."

Unimpressed, Sonya had continued to wind the phonograph.

"I'll play the music," she'd told him. "You can dance with Jody."

Where's Jody now? Will she be waiting for him out in his car?

Dan's slow-spoken question broke into her thoughts.

"How did you figure out where they were?"

"I called Mrs. Troy."

Sonya's voice sounded as if it were coming from a far distance — from someone else.

"She told me you'd rented this building."

"I rented it?" Dan stopped short. Obviously thinking hard.

"Whoever made the deal used my name. That way, if the garage was ever located, I'd be the fall guy. The same person succeeded in turning Alex against me by planting Mother's jewelry in my cabin."

Rain pounded even harder against the

metal roof. Sonya remembered what Mrs. Troy had said. A cashier's check. Easy to use his name.

"I know who did this, Sonya." His gaze fell again to the fur on top of the open box. "With this evidence and your help, I'll be able to prove it."

She wanted so badly to believe him. "Who do you think . . ." she started, but her words died away.

This is getting to be too much for me.

Dan began to explain.

"The trouble really started the day Alex began talking about selling out."

"Then Connie and Emil . . ." Sonya began, but once more she failed to complete her sentence.

Dan picked up the story again.

"I thought so, too, until this afternoon when Alma regained consciousness. She's refused to talk, not because she's afraid, but because she's involved."

He paused, then explained some more.

"You knew about the six thousand dollars her grandmother left her? I'm convinced Alma used this money to hire an arsonist to burn the warehouse."

"Alma? She wouldn't . . ."

Sonya's words were stopped by second thoughts. Someone could have taken advantage of Alma Steelman, of her intense devotion to Connie. It would've been easy to convince Alma that if Alex had cash, he wouldn't sell the house, and Connie, Emil, and her would be happy again.

Dan was watching her face change as she worked her way through what he was saying.

"Alma saw the fire as an easy solution to Connie's problem. The person she hired assured her he could solve everything if he had money enough to set up the arson and rent a place to store the inventory. Everyone knew Alma had this small nest-egg, and he might even have promised Alma that after the furs were sold, she would be rich herself."

What Dan was saying did make sense. Sonya had observed the total change that had occurred in Alma's behavior.

Alma had asked, "Is he sad because he did wrong things?" concerning John T. Rathmell's portrait the night she'd entered Sonya's room. Alma could have been referring to herself, to her own sense of guilt over her part in the robbery and fire.

And the amount Sonya had found hidden in the phonograph would be about half of Alma's inheritance.

She must have agreed to pay him half

before the arson and the other half when the job was completed.

Alma's partner had been willing to let her get by without making final payment, yet he continued to terrorize her, continued to look for the hidden cash.

Dan spoke again.

"Alma must have been very frightened when the sheriff came into the house after the fire. Then when Alex disappeared, she believed he'd been murdered. She evidently intended to make a full confession but made the mistake of telling her partner just what she was going to do."

If this were true, Alma was more of a victim than she was a co-conspirator. Sonya could accept the fact that Alma had been involved, but she wasn't sure who had instigated the whole procedure. She looked at Dan for a long time, aware that he might be telling her only a half-truth. After all, Dan seemed the one most likely to have given Alma instructions to call Mona Troy and make arrangements to rent this garage.

"Do you think Alma was carrying out orders from Emil?" Sonya asked hollowly.

"No, she was working with Melvin LaVett."

Sonya stared at him, too startled to reply, waiting for more.

"The way I figure it, LaVett was working in the barn, and Alma went there to talk to him. They got to arguing, and Alma told him she was going to tell the truth."

Astounded, Sonya began to take seriously the possibility of Melvin's guilt. Melvin had been the one who'd helped Alex search Dan's cabin, who'd led her uncle to Anna's ring and the other jewelry he'd placed there to frame Dan for the robbery. To Sonya, Melvin seemed no more than a kindly neighbor, a person with little to gain by befriending Alex. Now she began to waver. She could almost see Alma, sick with guilt, upset because Connie was upset, trudging across the field to talk to Melvin, to make things right again.

It could be possible.

When she and Dan had gone to the Bailey Place right after the fire to look for Alex, they'd found Alma there waiting for Melvin. Sonya recalled the afternoon she'd interrupted Alma talking to Melvin in Alex's workshed. She remembered how very distraught Alma had been that day and how quickly she'd left the moment Sonya had arrived. After the attack on Alma, Melvin had stayed at the Brighton house, and that very night the place had been thoroughly searched.

Dan had believed someone was following them on their first trip to this building.

Melvin LaVett?

After seeing how close Sonya was getting to the truth, Melvin could have shot at her to keep her from continuing her search for the arsonist.

"I've checked into LaVett's past," Dan said, as if trying hard to convince her.

"He's a drifter, moving from place to place. LaVett's one of those confidence men, preying upon people in need of assistance. Under the guise of helping Alex, he was in fact using him. He robbed Alex when he was ill and remained near, keeping watch for the next opportunity."

A voice spoke from the doorway behind them.

"Rathmell would really like you to believe that."

Dan and Sonya spun around, to see Melvin LaVett enter. Tall and lean in faded jeans and black rain-jacket, he stopped dead-still, glancing from one to the other, looking like a so-journer coming from some isolated woodland to take shelter from the storm.

"It's a good thing I followed you here, isn't it, Sonya?" he said, wide blue eyes holding earnestly to hers. "If I hadn't, you might have listened to his lies. Then you'd end up just like Alma."

His gaze roamed the room and came to rest on Dan.

"The furs aren't so easy to dispose of, are they? I guess you found that out. It's hard to make a deal for what they're worth. But I suppose by now you've decided to settle for what you can get."

He held out his arm. "Sonya, come on over here."

Sonya hesitated. A shiver passed over her. *Melvin looks so solid, like a loyal friend.*

But was that ability to inspire confidence what made him so very dangerous? Not knowing which of them to trust, Sonya remained frozen, the hammering of her heart blending with the rapid fall of rain against the roof.

From the belt beneath his jacket, Melvin took out a small revolver. He aimed it directly at Dan's heart.

"And now we'll all go talk to the sheriff."

"What are you going to do if Alma decides to talk?" Dan asked, almost matter-of-factly.

Melvin answered quickly

"Alma may never fully recover from that blow you gave her."

As he spoke, Melvin gestured with the gun barrel for Dan to move toward the door.

Dan looked at Sonya for a long time, causing LaVett to make twitching, 'get moving' motions at him with the gun. Then to her surprise and dismay, as if ready to admit he'd been caught, he moved with slow, measured gait toward the door.

Sonya watched, aghast.

Dan's pace changed with jolting suddenness. He lunged toward Melvin, steel-like fingers closing over the hand that held the gun. Forced upward, it fired, sending a bullet zinging into the ceiling.

Dan hurled Melvin's hand down across his knee. Expelled by pure force from Melvin's grasp, the revolver dropped and spun across the floor.

Melvin's fist struck hard against Dan's jaw. Dan reeled backward. At that same instant, Sonya reached the revolver.

Dan had managed to rise. Again he lunged at Melvin, but this time LaVett tore himself free from the grip. She could see the blurred image of Melvin's hand outstretched toward her and heard him call, "Sonya, give me the gun!"

For a moment she felt suspended, unable to act at all. She looked from one to the other. Then, in a split second decision, she reached Dan's side. She held her breath as she placed the gun into Dan's hand.

Face to face with the weapon, Melvin stared at her, at Dan, at the gun.

No one moved. Rain pelted against the tin roof. Trembling, Sonya waited, unsure of what Dan's next action would be. In the slow passage of moments, she prayed she'd made the right decision.

Dan, breathing hard, wiped the blood from his face.

"Let's go to the police station," he said. With his free hand, Dan reached back for Sonya, and they followed Melvin outside. They walked behind the man, close together, through the pouring rain.

CHAPTER 21

Uncle Alex, Dan, and Sonya stood on the front porch of the Rathmell mansion. A moment ago, when they'd walked up the steps, Dan's hand had reached for hers.

Alex strode away from them toward the door, then he turned back, his frosty eyes fastening on Dan.

"I'm hardly ever wrong," he drawled, that humorous tone to his voice, "but I guess I was this time. I'm glad, Dan. I'm glad I was wrong about you."

"I can't blame you for believing him. LaVett did everything he could to estrange us, to make me look guilty. And I didn't do very much to prevent it."

As Dan accepted Alex's outstretched hand, an understanding seemed to flash between them, a recognition of some old bond that had never been totally broken. Knowing Alex and Dan were reunited eased some of the dread Sonya felt over leaving them and returning to Boston.

"Melvin LaVett was skilled in getting a person's confidence," she said. "I didn't even suspect him."

"I should have," Alex responded. "I can see that now. Right from the first, he began undermining Dan. He even talked me into searching Dan's cabin, where he'd planted Anna's ring and scattered a few other trinkets he was sure I'd recognize."

"I never even thought to check up on him myself," Dan said, "not until he became interested in you, Sonya. Then I knew I had to find out more about him. I managed to get his fingerprints, and I hired a private investigator. I found out that LaVett worked for an elderly lady in California — one who died under very mysterious circumstances. I've a feeling that when Kansas is through with him, the California authorities are going to want him back there."

Before Sonya could reply, Connie and Emil came out of the house lugging large suitcases.

"How's Alma?" Sonya inquired.

"She's much better," Connie replied. "She's been wanting to see you."

"I'll drop by the hospital today."

"Poor Alma, she never once stopped to think about what she was doing," Connie opined. "She didn't do any of this for herself, but for me. That's just like her, isn't it?" She stopped to dab at her eyes, careful to look only at Sonya.

"Alma's never been in any trouble before," Sonya said gently. "I'm certain that'll be taken into consideration."

Connie turned to Emil.

"We're going to do everything we can for her, aren't we, Emil?"

Towering behind Connie, he nodded grimly.

"We're going to be staying down on Circle Street," Connie said, casting a sideways glance toward Alex. "If that's all right with you, Alex. But if Alma has to go to jail, then we're going to move right down to Lansing so we can be near her."

She lifted her suitcase again and led the way toward the waiting taxi.

Alex watched them depart.

"Too bad they can't all go to jail," he said, as they watched the cab turn toward Linnville. He started off inside, but stopped again, and in his crusty manner said, "Dan, you see if you can talk Sonya into staying here permanently. The three of us would have great fun fixing up the old house."

"Sonya surely wouldn't let us attempt it alone," Dan retorted, smiling. "Everything would look like that shed we built."

Both men laughed.

Sonya didn't have to return to Boston, she could just stay here in Linnville. Dan had always told her this was where she belonged. She looked from her uncle back to Dan, noting the sparkle that appeared in his black eyes.

"What about it?" Dan asked. "Would you consider marrying a Kansan?"

"Sure she would," Alex spoke up abruptly as he went into the house. "Anna did!"

"I love you, Sonya. Will you marry me? Soon?"

"I love you, too, Dan. And, yes, I'll marry you."

Happiness rushed over Sonya as, enfolded in Dan's arms, she added, "But on one condition. I want to get married right here in this house."

ABOUT THE AUTHOR

Loretta Jackson, author of the mystery novels, *Wake of Evil* and *Ensnared,* lives in Junction City, Kansas. She has co-authored, with her sister Vickie Britton, more than thirty books, mostly adventures and mysteries. In their Ardis Cole Mystery Series, archeologist Ardis Cole solves crimes in faraway locations, in Egypt, China, and Peru. The sisters travel to research each setting used in their work. Loretta Jackson's short stories have been published in the *Kansas Quarterly, The Family, My Weekly,* and the *Writer's Journal* and appear in three anthologies from Whiskey Creek Press — *Dead Man's Hand and The Devil's Hangman, The Bloody Knife,* and *No Longer Drifting.*

We hope you have enjoyed this Large Print book. Other Thorndike, Wheeler, and Chivers Press Large Print books are available at your library or directly from the publishers.

For information about current and upcoming titles, please call or write, without obligation, to:

Publisher
Thorndike Press
295 Kennedy Memorial Drive
Waterville, ME 04901
Tel. (800) 223-1244

or visit our Web site at:

www.gale.com/thorndike
www.gale.com/wheeler

OR

Chivers Large Print
published by BBC Audiobooks Ltd
St James House, The Square
Lower Bristol Road
Bath BA2 3SB
England
Tel. +44(0) 800 136919
email: bbcaudiobooks@bbc.co.uk
www.bbcaudiobooks.co.uk

All our Large Print titles are designed for easy reading, and all our books are made to last.